'You're *selling*?' The word was a gasp. 'But…you love this place. It's—' She was going to say *it's your home*, but the words caught. It wasn't any more, was it?

David still wasn't looking at her. 'You can't always keep the things you love, Annie.' The edges of his words were rough enough to negate the fact that he'd softened her name. They grated, like the way David's chair did as he pushed it roughly back to stand up. 'Sometimes you have to let them go in order to move on. That's life.'

He walked to the fridge and opened the door. Anne found herself staring at his back.

Fighting tears. He hadn't been talking about the house, had he?

THE BABY GIFT
A gift so special it's priceless

WISHING FOR A MIRACLE

Julia Bennett thinks she's come to terms with not being able to have a child of her own. But then she meets Mac, and would love for them to have a little family. But Mac knows that with Julia in it his life is complete…anything else is a blessing…

'We can make all our dreams come true
if we do it together.'
Julia's smile wobbled. 'You know what?'
'What?'
'I actually believe that.'

THE MARRY-ME WISH

Anne Bennett has been a mother already. She gave up her own childhood when her parents died and she had to bring up her baby sister Julia. Whilst she wouldn't change that for the world, she's finally living her own life. A talented surgeon, she's at the top of her game—but she knows there is one last, precious thing she can do for her sister…

When they came back from their honeymoon
Anne had a gift waiting for them. A promise.
'I want to be a surrogate mother for you,' she said.

But how will Anne's gorgeous ex-fiancé cope
when he sees her pregnant?

This month read the stories of both Bennett girls by favourite author Alison Roberts.
You'll laugh, cry, and be swept away on a heart-warming journey as both these young women find their happy-ever-after, whilst two sweet little bundles of joy steal your heart!

THE
MARRY-ME WISH

BY
ALISON ROBERTS

First published in Great Britain 2010
Large Print edition 2011
Harlequin Mills & Boon Limited,
Eton House, 18-24 Paradise Road,
Richmond, Surrey TW9 1SR

© Alison Roberts 2010

ISBN: 978 0 263 21717 9

Harlequin Mills & Boon policy is to use papers that are natural, renewable and recyclable products and made from wood grown in sustainable forests. The logging and manufacturing process conform to the legal environmental regulations of the country of origin.

Printed and bound in Great Britain
by CPI Antony Rowe, Chippenham, Wiltshire

Dear Reader

I'm not lucky enough to have a sister, but I do have an amazing daughter and many truly wonderful friends, so I'm well aware of what an astonishingly powerful thing the bond between women can be.

Friends, mothers and daughters...sisters. I started thinking about the kind of bond that might be created if it encompassed all of these possibilities. Could it be enough to overcome obstacles that seem impossible?

Neither Julia nor Anne Bennett envisages a future that involves children. Their reasons might be different, but the effect their convictions have on their relationships has the potential to be disastrous.

But Jules and Annie are more than simply sisters, and their bond is such that they will go to extraordinary lengths to help each other.

As far, even, as carrying a child for the one who can't.

That kind of bond is amazing all on its own, but I wanted to give these sisters even more. Men who love them for exactly who they are and futures that will allow all their dreams to come true.

Cherish the women in your life. The bond is magic.

With love

Alison

Alison Roberts lives in Christchurch, New Zealand. She began her working career as a primary school teacher, but now juggles available working hours between writing and active duty as an ambulance officer. Throwing in a large dose of parenting, housework, gardening and pet-minding keeps life busy, and teenage daughter Becky is responsible for an increasing number of days spent on equestrian pursuits. Finding time for everything can be a challenge, but the rewards make the effort more than worthwhile.

Recent titles by the same author:

NURSE, NANNY…BRIDE!
HOT-SHOT SURGEON, CINDERELLA BRIDE
THE ITALIAN SURGEON'S CHRISTMAS MIRACLE

CHAPTER ONE

'WE NEED you, Anne. I wouldn't ask but this is a real emergency.'

'What's up, Jeff? I thought you were in Theatre with a complicated valve replacement case.'

'I am. Got to scrub back in in a sec. We've got a theatre free up here but no surgeon. Six-year-old kid coming up from Emergency that I don't want to give to a registrar.'

'Trauma?'

'Hit by a car. Chest injuries, possible tamponade. There's an ED team coming up with him.'

'I'm onto it. Which theatre?'

'Three. They're setting up now. Are you sure, Annie? Your back all right?'

'I'll cope.'

A wry chuckle came down the phone line. 'As

long as you can still reach the table. I'll come in to assist as soon as I can leave my reg to close up.'

'I'll be fine, Jeff.'

Anne hit the 'save' button for the paper she'd been working on and pushed her chair back. It hadn't been so long since she would have leapt to her feet to respond to a call like this. Her brain was still fast enough but her body had somewhat different ideas.

Almost eight months pregnant. With twins, and her bump was impressive by anyone's standards. Her feet were swollen as well and she had permanent backache these days. Due to start a sabbatical break in just a week, Anne was using these last days to catch up on things there was never enough time for. Like journal reading to keep up with new developments in her field and departmental administration tasks, and her favourite—writing up papers to submit to specialist paediatric cardiovascular surgical journals. Already, her list of peer-reviewed papers was something to be proud of and the main goal of the upcoming break in her full on career was to recapture the joy of producing something to interest, if not challenge, like minds.

She couldn't turn away from this call, however. Not when the life of a six-year-old child was at stake.

The route from her office to the theatre suite only involved one flight of stairs so there was no point waiting for the elevator. Annoying to be so out of breath by the time she pushed open the fire-stop door in the stairwell but at least she was here before her patient.

A 'ping' announcing the arrival of an elevator sounded as Anne stepped through the swing door of the stairwell. The metal doors of the lift slid open by the time she was directly in front of them and there could be no doubt that this was the emergency she had been called upstairs for. The small space behind those doors was crowded.

A bed with a small person on it. A nurse holding bags of fluid steady on an IV pole. A doctor at the head of the bed holding an ambu-bag to assist breathing if necessary. A frame over the bed supported a defibrillator and other monitoring equipment. Another nurse was wedged in, carrying an oxygen cylinder, and leading the team was a consultant from the emergency department.

That consultant was someone Anne knew very well indeed but had never expected to see again. For just a heartbeat, she totally forgot what she was here for.

David?

He'd left St Patrick's hospital almost a year ago. He'd made no bones about being prepared to give up his senior position in the emergency department because it was the easiest way to end their relationship. Probably the only way they could finally tear apart a connection that was strong enough to be irresistible, but they had both known it was going nowhere.

How ironic that they should meet again like this.

For David to see her pregnant.

And in that same heartbeat, as his gaze lifted

to meet hers, Anne tried desperately to signal a message.

It's not what you think.

Oh, my God!

The shock was a physical thing. A kind of detonation somewhere behind his ribs that sent shockwaves rippling through his body. Unpleasant, electrical sort of jolts.

Anne was pregnant.

Enormously pregnant.

Glowing with it. Looking more beautiful than he ever remembered, with her rich, dark hair flowing over her shoulders and a loose, soft cotton top that caressed the huge bump of her stomach.

So it hadn't been that she hadn't ever wanted a family.

She just hadn't wanted one with *him*.

David didn't need to catch the flash of guilt in her eyes to confirm what was so blindingly obvious. Shock morphed instantly into a pain that he knew would become anger.

But not now.

'Keiran Burroughs, aged six,' he snapped. 'Hit by a car going approximately forty-five kilometres an hour. Flail chest, tension pneumothorax. Three-fifty mils drained so far. Cardiac arrhythmia—runs of VPBs. Arrested in ED prior to chest drain insertion and pericardiocentesis.'

The bed was moving forward as he spoke, underlying the urgency of getting this child into Theatre. Anne was assessing the boy visually, noting his lack of consciousness and pallor. She was also trying to read the figures on the monitor screens.

'X-rays?'

'I'll put them up while you get scrubbed.' He could see the anaesthetist waiting at the entrance to the theatre anteroom. As the bed was manoeuvred through the doorway, an alarm sounded from the life pack monitoring the heart rhythm. He was turning away from the surgeon as he spoke again.

'My shift has finished,' he said. 'I'd like to stay in Theatre if that's okay with you.'

Anne was also turning away, heading at speed towards the locker room.

'Of course,' was all she said. 'Fine by me.'

The bristles of the small, soap-impregnated brush were tough enough to make her skin sting. Or perhaps that was because she was scrubbing so hard and fast. Under her nails. Over and between her fingers. All the way up to her elbows.

Thank goodness she had something so automatic to do and something to think about that was so urgent it could override her reactions to seeing David again and knowing that he would be somewhere amongst the gowned and masked figures in Theatre with her.

Anne began rinsing her hands, angling them so that the water went from fingertip to elbow. Okay, maybe she wasn't being quite as successful as she thought. Had it only been this morning when she'd had coffee with her sister, Julia, and they'd been laughing? Excited about the imminent birth of these babies. Discussing names. Planning and dreaming for what lay ahead as they came so close to the culmination of a long-awaited dream.

Life could turn on a sixpence, couldn't it?

Happiness could be twisted and become unrecognisable. Get replaced with sadness and guilt and a tension she couldn't begin to analyse because there was someone far more important that David or herself or even her babies to consider right now. A small boy and his family whose lives had been derailed far more dangerously than her own.

This time, her success was complete. As a nurse tied the strings of her gown—not without difficulty given her new size—Anne Bennett had nothing on her mind other than the task that lay immediately ahead of her.

Saving the life of little Keiran.

It was unusual enough to have a woman who was only in her mid-thirties holding a senior position in a specialty as tough as this one. Even more unusual to see one working around the challenges presented by advanced pregnancy.

So advanced, it looked as if Anne might need to put her scalpel down and give birth at any moment.

David had only been gone for a year. Not quite a year, in fact, which meant that she must have become pregnant within weeks of him leaving the country.

Oh, anger was there all right. When he thought back to the sheer torment of uprooting himself. Trying to settle in a new place and a new job with the background misery of mourning a relationship that had died. Wishing it could have been different. Feeling displaced and...downright lonely.

And what had Anne been doing? Starting again. Sleeping with some other guy. Planning a family and a future. Disgust mixed with anger and hardened the stare David had fixed on the surgeon. Not that Anne was remotely aware of it, of course, and something else got mixed into that nasty emotional brew.

Jealousy. Not just for the fact that she'd been enjoying life while he'd been suffering. Or for the man she had chosen to be the father of her child. Right now, it was for her focus. Her career. The way she could be so totally absorbed in what she was doing that anything personal ceased to exist. Anne was completely free of the turbulent, painful thoughts David couldn't quite distract himself from. But it had always been like that, hadn't it? That focus. The passion that was more important than anything else in life.

If he was scrubbed in and right alongside the table he could have emptied his head and heart of anything other than this case. Even where he was, close to the anaesthetist at the head of the table where he was getting the best view without being in anyone's way, he could lose himself often enough to keep him from walking out of the operating theatre.

The tension was contagious. The difficulty in controlling the bleeding enough to see what damage lay inside that small chest. The time-critical period of starting cardiac bypass to allow repairs to the heart itself. David had to wait long enough to see what he'd been trying to deal with in the emergency department. The damage that the sharp ends of fractured ribs had caused to the vital organs they were supposed to protect. And then he had to see it though.

He was here because he had worked so hard already to stabilise this child and get him to Theatre. His determination to save the boy was still there and however irrelevant it now was, it was compelling to still be part of this equation. As though he could still make a contribution to the outcome. Staying long enough to know what that outcome was going to be was important. David had to wait and see if the heart could be restarted and whether the patchwork of repairs would be up to the job of supplying blood and oxygen under sufficient pressure to sustain life.

In between the dramatic start and finding out how this story would end was a lull as far as David was concerned, however. It was too hard to see into the chest cavity clearly enough to admire the tiny, neat sutures the surgeon was making. He could watch the monitors and follow any deterioration or improvement in the little boy's condition and he could listen to the verbal exchanges between the surgical team members and watch the instruments and equipment being used, but too much of his own head was free to wander. To stand back, like the observer he was physically. And how could he stay completely focused when he could hear Anne's voice giving quiet but clear instructions to her scrub nurse or registrar or asking for information on what the monitors were recording?

When he could see the shape of her body every time he looked up from the open square in the sterile, green drapes.

This was just so…wrong!

It had been *him* who'd wanted a family so much it had begun to poison what had been the love affair of his life.

Anne had been so adamant she couldn't give him what he wanted.

She'd been there and done that. Effectively been a mother from when she was still a child herself to her younger sister, Julia, when their mother had died shortly after Julia's birth.

They'd lived with a series of nannies in the household and she'd said she'd never wish that on a child of her own.

She'd fought hard to win the career of her dreams and no matter how much she loved David she couldn't give that up because she would be giving up too much of who she was.

But here she was. About to have a baby and, if she intended to keep her career, that child would be raised, to quite a large extent, by nannies. Or had she found a lover whose ambition was to be a house-husband?

Surely not. With a mind as sharp as Anne's, she needed someone she could talk to. Discuss her career with and medicine in general. The fascination she had with research and the ethical issues involved. The kind of animated, satisfying conversations she had always had with him.

When they hadn't been in each others arms, that was, indulging in a physical passion so powerful they had both known that being with anyone else could only be a compromise.

A compromise Anne had only too clearly been willing to make.

For someone else. Perhaps she'd planned it even before he'd made that final, excruciatingly painful decision to leave? Had the father of that baby already been waiting in the wings?

'Looking good,' he heard Anne say. 'I think we've done all we can. Let's start getting this lad off bypass.'

She sounded confident.She'd done all she could and, knowing Anne, it was probably enough.

David had done all he could as well, and not just for this little boy when he'd been under his care in the emergency department.

He'd done all he could to make their relationship work, hadn't he? And it hadn't been enough.

Suddenly sickened, David had to turn away. He didn't want to be here any longer. If he met Keiran's parents on the way out he would be able to tell them honestly that everything was going as well as they could hope for and that their son was in the best possible hands. He could go into Recovery in a little while and catch up with what was happening to this small patient.

And, in the meantime, he could spare himself the agony of seeing what had been going on in the life of the woman he loved since he'd removed himself from it. Spare himself the pain of hearing her voice.

Why on earth had he come back? Had he really thought that a three-month locum position here until he started a new posting overseas would be a good idea? It had seemed like a sensible punctuation mark in his life. He had loose ends to tie up that had been left. Just in case. Part of him hadn't been able to give up hoping that the separation might be all that had been needed to change Anne's mind.

If it hadn't, he'd be able to tick the box that said he'd done the right thing in leaving in the first place. That the misery of the last year had been worthwhile. He had achieved knowing he'd been right to leave in one fell swoop by simply catching sight of Anne. Killed that 'just in case' scenario stone dead. Now the problem was that he'd been through hell for no good reason whatsoever.

He'd given his heart to a woman who hadn't been honest with him. Hadn't actually been the woman he'd fallen in love with at all.

He could hate her for that. Hopefully.

'Sinus rhythm.' He could hear the triumph in Anne's voice behind him as she noted the normal activity in the small heart they'd just restarted.

He couldn't share the triumph. Utter defeat was dragging at his spirits. So much so that David left that operating theatre wishing fervently that he would never have to hear Anne Bennett's voice again.

CHAPTER TWO

'Don't cry, Annie. Please don't cry. You *never* cry.'

'It's hormones.' Anne gave a huge, gulping sniff and pulled back from her sister's fierce hug. 'It was just…he looked like he *hated* me, Jules.'

'He doesn't hate you. He just doesn't understand what's going on.'

'I should have told him.'

A tiny silence. Long enough to let Anne know that Julia agreed. But how could she have told David? His emails had been infrequent and, oh, so polite. The 'I hope everything's going as well for you as it is for me' kind of communication. He had been getting settled into a new job and a new country. Getting over her. There just hadn't been a good moment to drop in the 'I decided to be a surrogate mother for my sister and I'm pregnant with twins' kind of message.

'Here, come inside.' Julia was tugging Anne into the little house she shared with Mac on a bush-covered hillside overlooking the harbour. Into the kitchen with its old wooden cupboards and enamel sink and a wide window with a view to die for with one of the larger harbour islands centre stage. 'Sit down. I'm going to make us a cup of tea. Unless you'd like something stronger?'

Anne shook her head, grabbing a handful of tissues as she passed the box on the end of the bench. She'd been alcohol free for nine months now. They all had, in a kind of supportive pact, and this was no reason to break that pact. No reason to feel like the world had ended.

This time Anne blew her nose far more effectively. She wiped her eyes with more tissues and took a deep, steadying breath. Then she sat down, buried her face in her hands and groaned.

'It couldn't have been worse, you know? There we were with a critically ill child between us and he was looking at my bump and then he looked up and… Oh, *God*…it was like I'd slapped his face in public or something.'

'You just need to talk to him. You can tell him it was at least partly *his* idea all along.'

'What?' Startled, Anne raised her head to watch Julia as she busied herself at the bench, making the tea.

'Remember back when we were first talking about this whole surrogacy thing?' Julia poured boiling water into the teapot and put the lid on it. 'When you were trying to persuade me and Mac to accept your incredible wedding gift?'

'Yeah…I guess. Seems a long time ago.'

Julia brought the teapot and mugs to the table. 'You said that Dave had told you over and over again that you could be missing the most amazing experience of your life by not wanting to be a mother. That you would regret it one day.'

Anne sighed as she nodded slowly. 'And I told you that part of all that angst had taken root and while it hadn't changed my mind about trying to juggle a career with being a parent, he could be right about the experience of being pregnant and giving birth.'

'So there you go.' Julia's smile was encouraging, albeit still worried. 'You said you'd found the perfect compromise. You get the whole experience and get to watch babies growing up but you can be an aunty and not a mum.' She bit her lip. 'Do you still feel like that?'

'Of course I do. Why wouldn't I?'

'Because you've seen David again and you're so upset. You still love him, don't you?'

'Of course I do,' Anne repeated, her tone hollow. 'I'll always love him but it would never have worked. He's desperate for a family and I can't give him that. We both knew it wouldn't be enough, not having one. He would have ended up resenting me.'

'I thought that about Mac and look what happened.'

'Mac adores you.'

'Maybe David feels the same way about you.'

'I don't think so.' Anne could feel her face

settle into grim lines as she picked up the mug of tea Julia had poured. 'If he did, he wouldn't have agreed it was time to pull the plug. He wouldn't have gone off to start a new life on the other side of the globe. He wouldn't have sent horrible, polite emails that sounded like they were coming from a stranger. And he certainly wouldn't have been looking at me today as if I'd just stuck a knife in his heart.'

'Oh, Annie…'Julia leaned over the corner of the table to give her sister another hug and, as she did so, a door banged from outside the kitchen.

'Is that Annie's car out there?' The delight in the male voice changed to concern as Mac entered the kitchen. 'Oh, no,…what's happened? Are you all right, Annie?'

'Yes, I'm fine,' Anne said, and burst into tears again.

Mac was by her side in an instant, his face stricken. She could feel his concern wrap around her like a blanket. It was partly the close bond they'd made in the last year but she could feel another part. Professional concern. As a paramedic, like Julia, he was assessing her physical condition. Looking for reasons for this highly unusual breakdown.

'It's hormones, that's all,' she sobbed. 'Take no notice of me.'

The box of tissues materialised beside her on the table and, as she reached for a fresh handful, Anne could see Mac looking at his wife with a question in his eyes.

'David turned up at the hospital today,' Julia told him. 'He saw Anne but she didn't get a chance to tell him why she's pregnant.'

'Ohhh…' Mac dragged out another chair and sat down right beside Anne. He squeezed her arm. 'And you think he thinks you've gone from breaking up with him to start a family with some other bloke.'

If Mac could see it so clearly it was a no-brainer, wasn't it? She *should* have told him. Why had she been so stupid? Because she'd been stamping so hard on any of those fantasies where he turned up in her life again and said he couldn't live without her? She had been trying to be realistic. Trying not to expect to ever see him again. Getting on with her life. Giving the only other people in the world she loved this much of a gift.

'Well, that's easily fixed.' Mac sounded satisfied. 'You just need to talk to him. And if that's too hard, I could talk to him. Bloke to bloke, you know.'

Anne shook her head. 'It won't help. He'll think if I could get pregnant for you guys I should have done it for him. That's why I never told him in the first place. He wasn't meant to know anything about this.'

A silence fell over the small group.

'You know...' Julia sounded tentative. 'There could be another way around this.' She had been staring into the depths of her mug but now she looked up at Anne. 'I could give you what you've given me and Mac. A...chance at a family.'

Both Mac and Anne were staring at her. Anne felt a fond smile tug at her lips. They were so different. She was tall and dark and Julia was like a little imp with spiky blonde hair. And thanks to the unusual circumstances of their childhoods, not to mention the trauma of going through the hysterectomy Julia had had to have when she had only been in her early twenties, they were far closer than most sisters ever got to be. She loved Julia with all her heart but that familiar, determined light glowing in her eyes right now would have to be dampened.

'I don't think so, hon,' she said gently.

'I'm going to be at home with the twins.' Julia was undeterred by the soft warning in Anne's tone. 'I'm happy to be giving up work to be a full-time mum. Couldn't be happier. I'll be at home for years and years and what could be better than having cousins around for our two?'

'A kind of blended family…' Mac was absorbing her idea. 'You know, it might work. Jules is an aunty so it wouldn't be like having nannies that didn't love your kids as much as you do. She's going to be the best mum in the world, I can guarantee that.'

Mac was smiling. Anne could see the way his

gaze was drawn irresistibly to Julia's. The way it held.

She knew that look. That kind of bond you could only get with the love of your life.

The kind of bond she and David had had. Way back. Before there had been any question of just how disparate they saw their future paths in life.

She missed that bond.

Here she was, sitting with the people she loved most in the world. About to have an experience they'd all been dreaming about for so long, and she'd never felt so utterly miserable.

So lonely.

It was too much. Something deep inside her snapped.

She pushed her barely touched mug of tea away so sharply it slopped onto the table. Her voice came out high and tight.

'I don't *believe* this,' she said. 'You're both starting to sound exactly like David used to. Pressuring me into doing something I don't want to do by finding ways around it.'

She pushed herself to her feet, shaking her head with an angry gesture. 'This is it. A one-off! Why won't anyone understand that?'

'We do understand,' Julia said urgently. 'I'm sorry, Annie. It was just—'

Anne cut her off. The anger and misery were coalescing now. A volcano that had to erupt.

'You don't understand anything,' she said bitterly. 'How could you? You have *no* idea how hard it's been to do my job ever since I got pregnant. Feeling rotten with morning sickness… being tired all the time. Having backache that's been killing me every time I've been in Theatre for months and months.'

Julia's face had gone pale. Mac was standing up, looking unsure of whose side he should go to. His wife or the angry pregnant woman who was shouting at them both?

Anne spared him having to make the decision. 'I'm leaving,' she announced. 'And I don't want to talk to either of you right now so don't try and stop me.' She got to the door but had to turn back for a parting shot. 'You might be happy to give up your job to be a mother,' she told her sister. 'That's great. Absolutely peachy. But that's *you*, not me. I'm *not* happy to give up mine. I thought I'd manage a lot better than this but, if I'm being honest, it's been extremely hard and I'm not doing it again. For you *or* David.'

Julia's face had crumpled now, on the verge of tears. Could this day get any worse? Anne closed her eyes.

'Look…I'm sorry.' She opened her eyes again and took a deep breath. 'Blame it on the hormones. I chose to do this for you and I'm happy about it, honestly. Presenting David with a baby isn't going to fix what went wrong. It's…like you guys. A family has to be a bonus, not something to patch up a relationship that's come apart.'

Somehow they were all within hugging range again now. There were tears but the knowledge that they would all get through this and come out stronger on the other side.

It was Anne who pulled away. 'I really do need to go,' she told them. 'I've got a ton of stuff I have to get done. Nesting urge or something probably but I really do need to get to the super-market and buy enough toilet paper to last the next six months.'

Shaky laughter was following her as she headed for the door.

'It's bad luck that David's happened to come back at this particular point,' she added by way of farewell, 'but I can deal with it.' She smiled to prove it. 'You're both right. I just need to talk to him.'

Weird that having an emergency department crowded with sick and injured people and a team of medical staff depending on his skills to make sure it was running smoothly enough that no one fell through any cracks had often seemed too stressful to be enjoyable.

But this was great! Perfect.

'Get Security to cubicle three,' he instructed the receptionist.

'Set up the trauma room for incoming patients from that MVA,' he told a hovering nurse. 'And

Resus 1. Page the team. We're expecting three status 1 and 2 patients.'

David took just a moment to survey the spaces on the whiteboard beside the main triage area. 'We need to juggle beds,' he said to the registrar by his side. 'I want Resus 2 clear if possible. Has Cardiology assessed that patient yet?'

'No.'

'Chase them up. What about Orthopaedics for that neck of femur?'

'She's gone to X-Ray.'

'Head injury in cubicle seven?'

'Gone for a scan.'

More staff were already streaming into the department in response to their pagers.

'Incoming trauma?' a young anaesthetist queried.

David gestured towards the doors where ambulances could be seen, red and blue lights still flashing, turning to back up to the loading bay. With a nod to another knot of ED staff, already gowned and gloved, he moved to help intercept the incoming stretchers.

For the next hour they were all too pushed to do any more than manage the most critical cases under their care. Troubleshooting bleeding that couldn't be controlled. Fluid resuscitation. Airway management. Chest drains and fracture management. A fragile cardiac case that came hot on the heels of the road-accident victims. A baby with febrile seizures and a hysterical young mother whose sobbing could be heard from the other side of the department.

Chaos. Controlled but exhausting.

Yes. This was great.

David was every bit as focused as Anne had been in Theatre yesterday. Totally committed to doing his job to the best of his ability. No worries about getting distracted, although somewhere in the back of his mind he knew an account was being registered and that there would be a price to pay for this escape.

Another virtually sleepless night, probably, with the kind of emotional turmoil that was just as draining as running a large emergency department at full tilt, but he was quite prepared to pay that price.

And, with a bit of luck, by the time this shift ended, he'd be too whacked to even care.

Making another visit to the paediatric intensive care unit when his working day *was* finally over was pushing things a bit too far, really, but David could already feel that odd kind of calm that came when all reserves of adrenaline were depleted.

The worst that could happen would be that he could find Anne in the unit, which would be unwelcome but quite manageable. Thanks to the windows in the doors and the fact that little Keiran's space was almost opposite those doors, he would be able to see her before she could see him. He could simply turn around in that case and come back another time. It would be slightly more awkward if she arrived while he was there but, hey, it was a crowded area. As long as he avoided any direct eye contact, he would be fine.

After all, what could she possibly do or say that would be any worse than yesterday?

'You've just missed Dr Bennett,' a nurse told him helpfully as he neared the desk. 'She can't be far away and she'd be able to update you better than me. Would you like me to page her?'

'Good heavens, no.' David gave the pretty, young nurse his most charming smile. 'I'm sure she's even keener than I am to get home and put her feet up.'

'Mmm.' The nurse's cheeks had gone very pink. 'It must be hard being at work when you get to that stage of pregnancy.'

David's smile felt as though it had been flicked off with a switch. 'I'll read the notes, if that's okay. He's looking good from here.'

The nurse nodded. 'Dr Bennett seemed very happy and she spent a bit of time reassuring his mother. Poor woman… She's a single mother and he's her only child and I don't think she's even closed her eyes since Keiran arrived in here.'

David followed her line of vision to the woman who sat beside the small boy attached to the bank of monitoring equipment. Lines of anguish were ingrained on her face and her eyes were deeply shadowed. She looked up, as though sensing the attention she was under, and David smiled at her. A very different kind of smile this time. Sympathetic. Encouraging. One that put him in her corner.

'I'll have a chat to her when I've caught up on the notes,' he told the nurse.

'See if you can persuade her to go to the cafeteria or something and get a meal. She needs a break.'

David was happy to take on the mission. Having read all the documentation and reassured that Keiran was doing extremely well, he was able to add to his mother's reassurance.

'Looks like he might even come off the ventilator tomorrow and then they'll be able to lighten the sedation and let him wake up. He'll need you even more then, so it's important that you look after yourself. Rest. Eat.' David softened the commands with another smile. 'Doctor's orders.'

Keiran's mother nodded but she sounded vague. 'I'll go to the cafeteria,' she promised. 'I think I know where it is.'

'Why don't you come with me now? I'll be walking right past it to go home and if you go now you won't miss out on their macaroni cheese. It's legendary.'

'Is it?' For the first time, David saw a hint of a smile. 'That's our favourite, me and Kerry.'

'You'll be able to tell him how good it is, then. Something for him to look forward to once he's up on the ward. Come on.'

'He won't wake up, will he?' Her frown deepened as she reached out to touch her son. 'While I'm gone?'

'No chance. He's being kept asleep until he can breathe properly for himself. And he has his nurse right here. She'll be with him the whole time.'

'I will,' the nurse assured her. 'And I know where you'll be. I can send for you if anything changes.'

'Okay, then.' This time David received a real

smile. One that said he was trusted. 'Let's go now, before I change my mind.'

The busy part of the day was well over now and the lighting in the corridors was dim. Visitors would start arriving for the evening hours soon but this was a hiatus where routine activity had ceased and, apart from emergencies, the hospital would rest until tomorrow. All was calm, including David. His critical patient from yesterday was doing well, he had avoided any unpleasant confrontation with the woman he didn't want to see and any moment now he would be leaving the hospital grounds and heading for the safety of his own home.

The turn-off to the cafeteria was not far from a back entrance to the emergency department, which suited David very well. He needed to collect his jacket and briefcase and indulge a long-ingrained habit of walking through the department after his shift finished to make sure that it was still running smoothly. That he hadn't left anything undone that could have repercussions later on.

The couple standing against the wall opposite the door that led through the orthopaedic department and into Emergency didn't notice David going past because they were too wrapped up in each other.

But David noticed them.

The man was tall, dark and good looking and he wore the overalls that advertised he was part of an elite helicopter rescue team. The kind of paramedic that David had enormous respect for as an emergency consultant. Taller than the woman beside him, he was looking down at her. Or maybe he was looking at his hand which was resting on the bulge of her pregnant stomach. His fingers were splayed and his expression suggested that he was very comfortable doing this. That he was experiencing the kind of delight and wonder at what he was feeling beneath his hand that…a father would experience connecting with his unborn child.

Anne was watching this stranger and she had a dreamy half-smile playing on her lips. They were both standing very still and all that mattered to either of them was the baby inside her.

He only saw the tableau for a heartbeat. Or maybe it was two before he could wrench his gaze away, but there was no way of erasing it from his brain as David shoved the fire stop doors open and walked towards his office as though the hounds of hell were nipping at his heels.

Jealousy gripped him, hot and bitter. They had looked so content. So *happy.*

So much for all those impassioned conversations with Anne where she'd pleaded the importance of her career. The importance of a mother being more than part time. The fact that she worked with children and gave so much of herself to her patients that she would not have enough left for any of her own.

Lies, all of it. But he'd believed her. *Trusted* her.

At least the way forward was crystal clear now.

He would put his house on the market. He had

a couple of late shifts to get through but then he had the two days off and could start tidying up the property. Uninhabited for some time since his tenants had broken their lease and left, the garden was seriously overgrown and there were numerous maintenance jobs that needed doing urgently. He could organise a team of workmen and get everything sorted and then get it sold. He would give notice that he couldn't complete this locum for personal reasons. He'd tie up every damned loose end he could think of and then he'd be out of here.

And this time there would be no coming back.

Oh…Lord! Had that been *David*?

She only saw his back as the man pushed through the doors but, yes, Anne was sure it had been.

He'd seen her, standing here with Mac. A chance meeting after Mac had delivered a patient to Emergency and was heading for a vending machine for a snack and Anne had been coming back from delivering an urgent test to Pathology. The babies must have sensed it was time for her to be heading home because while they were normally quite quiet while she was busy working, they had chosen that moment to have a wrestling match or something in her womb.

Both Julia and Mac loved to feel their babies moving. It was a treat. A gift that Anne had been delighted to share. It was usually something kept very private but tonight the opportunity had presented itself like an apology for her outburst yesterday. Any resentment of the discomforts of this pregnancy had been transitory and Anne had been feeling terrible at leaving Mac and Julia worried.

And, yes, in the back of her mind had been the thought she might duck into the emergency department and try talking to David so the chance to stand here for a few minutes and gather courage had been welcome.

Maybe it wasn't too late.

'I need to go,' she told Mac. 'There's something I want to do before I head home.'

'Sure thing.' Mac took his hand off her stomach. 'Thanks for that. I'll be able to tell Jules we've got a couple of little rugby players in there. She'll be sorry she missed it.'

'I'll see her tomorrow. We're going shopping.' Anne threw a smile over her shoulder as she moved towards the doors. 'Have you any idea of how much your wife is spending at the baby shops?'

Mac grinned. 'Tell her to go for gold. Nothing but the best will do.'

Anne's smile vanished as the doors closed behind her. She went directly for the office area the consultants shared before she could lose the small amount of courage she had.

But David was nowhere to be seen.

She went into the department, trying to keep the urgency out of both the way she moved and spoke.

'Is Dr Earnshaw around, by any chance?' she asked the triage nurse.

'He just left. Did you need him for something in particular?'

'No… Um...' Anne tried to stop herself looking towards the exit in case she saw him. If she was honest with herself, there was an element of relief in finding she had missed him. It would have been bad enough anyway but in the wake of him seeing her in what could only have appeared a compromising position with Mac it would have been much worse. 'I was just going to update him on the little boy he treated yesterday. The one hit by the car.'

'Oh…Keiran. How's he doing?'

'Really well. Could you pass that on, maybe, when Dr Earnshaw's in tomorrow? Or…tell him to page me.'

The nurse was nodding but clearly hadn't noticed the way Anne clenched her fists at her final words and she couldn't know how her heart was hammering at the thought of hearing David's voice on the phone. She was distracted, in any case, by the arrival of a stretcher. Someone with a neck collar and padding in place that suggested a spinal injury.

Anne left the department. It should feel like a

reprieve but, instead, she could feel a new tension in the wake of realising how fast David must have left the building.

Was he avoiding her?

Quite probably, she decided the next day when several pager messages went unanswered.

He was nowhere to be seen when she found an excuse to go into the emergency department on her way home the day after that either but Anne hesitated before making a query about when he was next rostered on.

If she started asking questions, where would she stop?

Would someone know why he was here at all? Or how long for? Where he was living?

He'd leased out his house long term when he'd left so he couldn't have gone back to the fabulous property he'd inherited from his mother. That huge old house in the exclusive, leafy suburb that Anne was as familiar with as she was with her own home.

How weird would that feel, to come back to

the city you'd lived in virtually your whole life but not be able to go home?

It probably paled into insignificance compared to seeing the woman you'd loved, who'd sworn she never wanted children, looking ready to give birth at any moment.

She was getting used to the startled looks people gave her belly—as though it was a miracle she could still function with such a massive bump. Anne's smile was wry. Just as well they hadn't decided to implant all the embryos and she wasn't pregnant with triplets.

It was becoming seriously difficult to fit behind the steering-wheel of her car now. Maybe she shouldn't be driving any more? Imagine what could happen in even a minor collision? Fortunately it was only a short drive to her inner-city cottage and when she arrived safely she threw her car keys into a drawer and shut it firmly. From now on she was going to walk or take a taxi.

She'd cut her hours at the hospital for the next

few days too and then she was going to turn into the world's biggest couch potato.

And maybe…hopefully…she would be able to get her head around David's reappearance in her life and decide what to do about it.

She was overdoing things. No wonder she felt too emotionally fragile to cope with talking to him.

And no wonder her back was aching so much.

Six hours later, just after midnight, her backache still hadn't eased and that was when Anne felt the first contraction.

She rang Julia and Mac immediately.

'I just had a contraction,' she said tersely. 'Damn it! It's way too early.'

'You're a little bit over thirty-six weeks,' Julia said, clearly struggling to sound calm. 'That's not early for twins. You'll be fine, Annie. Mac's on a night shift. I'll ring him and then I'm on my way. It'll take me a good thirty minutes to get into town, though, so if the contractions speed up, you should get yourself to hospital. Don't drive. Call a taxi.'

'Ah…' Anne could feel the grip of a new contraction starting already. She could also feel an ominous trickle of fluid down her legs.

'Annie?' Julia's voice lost any pretence of calm. 'Are you all right?'

'I think…my waters just broke.'

'Forget the taxi.' She could hear Julia's sharp intake of breath. Could almost hear her sister's mind click into professional mode, so she wasn't surprised at the authority in her voice when she spoke again. Crisply this time.

'I'm going to call an ambulance for you. Hang in there, Annie. Help's on its way.'

CHAPTER THREE

THIS was a first.

In all his years as an emergency physician, David had faced just about everything. He had dealt with terrible trauma and heart-breaking tragedy. He had seen mistakes happen or grappled with the futility of attempting the impossible. He had even managed violent situations when his own life might have been at stake.

But he couldn't face this!

This pregnant woman on the stretcher with the extra paramedic in the crew. One that was holding her hand to advertise their connection as she was wheeled through the doors of the emergency department. David bent his head over the notes he'd been reading, pretending to concentrate but aware of little more than the way his heart rate had accelerated.

'This is Anne Bennett,' he heard the crew leader tell the triage nurse. 'Thirty-six-year-old primigravida. She's thirty-six weeks pregnant with twins. Waters broke approximately fifteen minutes ago and contractions are now three to four minutes apart.'

Twins?

Good grief. An instant family. David couldn't help looking up. The head of the triage nurse was turning now. Looking for him. David found his own head turning. Looking for someone else. Anyone else would do.

Staff numbers were at a minimum, of course. After midnight on a weeknight, things didn't generally get that busy. Three consultants were more than enough, with their registrars and the nursing staff. But one team was on a meal break and the other consultant was in the trauma room, dealing with a lacerated artery on a young man who'd put his fist through a window.

Which left him. Or a registrar.

'Any problems with the pregnancy so far?' the nurse was asking.

'No.' It was the man who answered the question. 'Everything's been perfect.'

David almost snorted. Perfect? Was that what Anne had told him? Perfect relationship. Perfect pregnancy. About to produce a perfect little family.

Yes. A junior doctor could handle this. All that was needed was a quick check on the stage of labour, filling in all the admission paperwork and a transfer to the maternity department.

Where *was* his registrar?

'Dr Earnshaw?'

David turned back, still trying to think of some way to escape this situation. He had to. He was too involved. It would be unethical to examine this woman and…and he didn't want to. He didn't want to have to touch her. Or see parts of her body that had haunted his life for what seemed like for ever.

But he had to turn back. He had to look at Anne and then he had to take a step closer because he'd never seen her look quite like this.

Pale. Frightened.

She tried to smile at him in a show of bravado but her knuckles were white where she held her companion's hand and her eyes were huge. Fastened on his, and there was a plea there.

She needed help.

She was asking for *his* help.

'Resus 1,' he ordered, his voice firm enough to disguise an inward groan. 'And page Obstetrics. Get them to bring an incubator down here as well, just in case. Actually, make that two.'

Thirty-six weeks wasn't that much of a worry in terms of prematurity for a single baby but these were twins who were likely to have lower birth weights anyway. Plus, he knew nothing about this pregnancy. He hadn't even known it existed, dammit. Was it unreasonable to feel so hurt by that? He'd been starting over, for God's sake. Struggling to let go of the past and start a new life. Surely it would have been courteous at the very least to inform him of something that might have allowed him to move forward with a semblance of enthusiasm?

The flurry of activity that followed his instructions gave David a minute or two to collect himself. Anne was taken into the well-equipped resuscitation area and transferred onto the bed. Nurses helped peel off extra clothing and blankets. A blood-pressure cuff was wrapped around her arm. Someone was sent to find an Entonox cylinder.

David donned a gown and gloves. Professional accessories that somehow helped him switch off the personal issues he had with this case. He could do this. He had to, because no matter how hurt and angry he was at the way he'd been treated, he cared about Anne. He would never forgive himself if he didn't make sure she received the best assessment and treatment he was capable of providing. An IV line was a priority. So was some form of foetal monitoring. Checking the position of the babies and how far along her cervix was in dilatation.

'Ohhhh!' Anne's groan cut through the air, ripping into David and threatening to undermine his resolve. 'Oh, God... *Mac...*'

'It's okay, love.' The big man with the tousled

dark hair had his arm around her shoulders as Anne leaned forward in her sitting position, drawing her legs up so that she could hang onto her knees. 'You're doing great.'

'Where's the Entonox?' David picked up the blue plastic kidney dish that contained everything he needed to start an IV line, doing his best to stamp on the flash of resentment he was feeling towards this Mac. The way he was holding Anne. The kind of anxiety on his face that every man would have if the woman he loved was in such pain.

'Here.' A nurse held the tubing attached to a large cylinder that had just been wheeled through the curtains. 'I was on the phone to Obstetrics. The registrar is tied up with a forceps delivery. They've paged a consultant but it'll be twenty minutes before they can get here.'

It was looking more and more likely that Anne was going to have her babies here. Especially given the way she kept shifting position, looking restless and irritable, which could well indicate an advance into the second stage of labour. She pushed away a hand that was offering her the mouthpiece to the inhaled pain relief.

'It's nitrous oxide,' David reminded her. 'A fifty-fifty mix of—'

'I know what Entonox is,' Anne snapped. She dragged in a breath as her contraction eased.

'I'm going to have a feel of your tummy while you're between contractions,' David warned her.

'Fine.' Anne closed her eyes.

The nurse pulled up the nightshirt Anne was wearing. An oversized T-shirt that he didn't recognise, but when had she ever worn clothing to bed when he'd been around?

The feel of her skin was all too familiar but at least her abdomen had never felt remotely like this. Hard and firm and stretched to what seemed like breaking point. Full of lumpy shapes. An elbow there. A foot here. David remembered seeing Mac with his hands exactly where his own were now. Entranced by feeling all those tiny limbs moving. He wasn't feeling any movement at the moment.

'Have we got a Doppler here?' he asked his registrar.

'I think so.'

'Maybe you could find it, then,' David heard himself snapping.

He looked up to catch the way his junior colleague's eyebrows rose. And no wonder. A flash of temper was disturbingly unlike the way he treated the people he worked with. David offered a quick smile. 'I'd like to check on the foetal heart rates after contractions.'

'Is something wrong?' Anne had picked up on the exchange.

'Not that I can pick up,' David reassured her. 'Have you had a scan recently?'

'I've been getting them weekly. To check on the growth rate. It's been within normal range and they're pretty even in size.'

'Do you know the presentation?'

'Cephalic-cephalic.'

'Good.' The babies were both presenting head first. 'As normal as it gets, then.'

Anne groaned again. 'Mac, where's Jules? She's supposed to *be* here.'

Yes. Definitely irritable. The sooner he could check on her dilatation the better. David moved towards the end of the bed.

'She's on her way,' Mac told Anne.

'Oh...*God*...' Anne flopped back onto her pillows. 'I don't believe this. I must have been mad to offer to have these babies for you. This *hurts*.'

David stiffened at her words. She had 'offered' to have babies for this man? She made it sound as if she hadn't actually wanted to. Ha! No surprises there.

'Try the Entonox.' His tone was cool. 'The pain relief can be very effective. I need to check your cervix, if that's all right.'

Anne gave an incredulous huff. She didn't want it to be him doing this any more than he did. 'Just get on with it, David. I'd rather get this over with as soon as possible. If that's *all right*.'

It was fine by him. Even making allowances for how women could lash out at people they cared most about during labour, her sarcasm had hit home. This was intolerable. And about to get worse. As David lifted the sheet, Anne muttered something that made him pause.

'Sorry?'

'I said, Jules was right. This is just as much your fault as Mac's.'

'Oh?' The distraction was all he needed to be able to continue this examination. His hands did what they needed to do while his brain focused on his patient's extraordinary statement.

'You said I'd be missing one of life's great experiences by never giving birth,' Anne said. 'So here I am. And...and right now I wish I wasn't.'

That made two of them. 'You're fully dilated,' he informed Anne. 'You can start pushing any time you feel the urge.'

David straightened to find he was being stared at by the man still holding Anne's hand.

'You're David?' He looked both startled and sympathetic. As though he knew a little too much about how Anne's ex might be feeling in this situation. What had Anne told him? That she'd had to end their relationship because she had no desire to have a family with him? But that she was prepared to go through it for *him*?

David glared at him. 'And you are?'

'Mac.' A fleeting grin. 'Annie's brother-in-law.'

David's jaw dropped. So did those of the nursing staff. Before anyone could say anything, however, the curtains parted and a small figure dashed into the resus area.

'Annie!'

'Jules. About time, kid. You nearly missed the action. Ohhh…' Anne extended her hand. 'I'll try some of that Entonox now, thanks.'

Now Anne had a figure on both sides of her bed. Her sister and her brother-in-law. David was missing something here. Something big.

'I rang Emily,' Julia was telling Mac. 'She'll be here any minute.'

'Who the hell is Emily?' It was about to get absurdly crowded in here, given that a new arrival was pushing a large incubator into the space.

David had the feeling he was losing his grip on reality. Assumptions were being splintered but he didn't know how to put the pieces into a picture that would be comprehensible.

'She's Annie's O and G consultant,' Julia told him. 'Assisted fertility specialist and a friend. She's been managing this pregnancy all along and she wants to be present for the birth. Oh, my God!' Anne's sister's eyes widened. 'David—it's *you*!'

'I want to push,' Anne announced. *'Ohhh!'*

However complicated this situation was, the birth itself was apparently going to be straight-forward. Within minutes, David found himself controlling the descent of a tiny head covered with crinkly, dark hair, keeping it flexed until crowning to protect Anne from tearing.

Waiting for the next contraction, David was aware of yet another arrival at this bedside. A female voice overrode the reassurance and en-couragement Anne was receiving from both Mac and Julia.

'I'm Emily Scott,' the woman said. 'O and G. Need a hand?'

'We're good for now.' David could see the first shoulder appearing. This wasn't the moment to hand over management, even to a specialist already familiar with the patient.

'Fabulous.' The voice was being directed at someone behind him now. 'Can we get another bed in here, please? I'd like the mother to be able to get some skin contact with these infants.'

David's breath caught somewhere in his chest. His brain registered the odd statement from the most recent arrival but he couldn't process it because he was stunned by the fact he was now holding Anne's newborn baby.

'It's…' His voice sounded raw. He had to blink and then look up from the baby who was drawing its first breath to catch Anne's gaze. To make contact. 'It's a boy.'

He began to lift the baby to put it onto her chest but Anne was shaking her head. With tears streaming down her face, she still produced a wobbly smile.

'Give him to his mother,' she said.

Julia was crying as well. She held out her arms and a nurse draped a clean towel across them. David placed a wriggling and healthily pink baby carefully onto the towel and Julia gathered him into her arms, lifting him to nestle against the only available skin she had, where the top of her shirt was unbuttoned.

'We need another bed,' Emily ordered. 'Let's make some room, people. Any unnecessary staff can leave.' With gloves on, she was moving to check Anne's belly and she had a Doppler to assess the remaining baby's condition.

It was probably just as well she was taking over the management of this birth because David was staring at Julia, the pieces of this puzzle finally falling into place.

This was a surrogate pregnancy.

Anne hadn't replaced him with someone she wanted to have a family with. Fragments of distant conversations were appearing in his memory. Julia had been diagnosed with endometrial cancer in her early twenties. Early stage, thank goodness, but it had meant having a hysterectomy, and dealing with the certainty of never being able to have children had been difficult to work through. There had been a disastrous relationship as well, years ago, when he had first dated Anne and he'd been envious of the close bond between the sisters. And a little put out by having to wait his turn for her time and attention.

Anne was doing something for her sister she'd never wanted to do for herself. Extraordinary. Impressive even, but David wasn't going to try and analyse the turmoil of his own reaction right now. Not when the Doppler was relaying the rapid 'clop clop clop' of an unborn baby's heartbeat and advertising that there were far more important things he should be thinking about.

'Do you want an oxytocin infusion set up?' he asked the obstetrician.

'Set it up, but we won't use it immediately. Let's wait and see if we get a spontaneous onset of some more contractions. Baby sounds like she's coping. How are you doing, Anne?'

'Um…I'm good…I think.' Anne was watching her sister holding the baby. Mac had moved to that side of the bed and he was holding Julia as she held the infant. Everybody seemed to be crying and David could feel an ominous prickle behind his own eyes. He cleared his throat and reached for some clamps.

'Would the father like to cut the cord?'

'Sure.' Mac was grinning. And sniffing. David caught his glance and read a trace of something that could have been embarrassment there. Because he was being so emotional in public or was it because he was the father here and not David? Whatever it was—joy or sympathy—he could feel a connection to this stranger who was realising his dream of having a family against what had probably seemed impossible odds. Besides, he was obviously a nice guy. Impossible not to like him instinctively.

'Scissors are on the trolley, mate. Cut here, just between these clamps.'

Somehow, another bed was being slotted into this small area. Julia climbed onto it and unselfconsciously bared her chest to hold her tiny son.

'Perfect Apgar,' Emily announced a minute later. She swivelled back to the other bed. 'Now, Anne. Let's have another look at you and see how things are shaping up for number two.'

He could have escaped before the arrival of the second baby. If a serious case had come into the department, he would certainly have made the effort to squeeze past the extra bed and all these people and leave them to it.

Part of him wished a nurse would put her head around the edge of the curtain and summon him to somewhere he was actually needed but he couldn't just leave. Not while Anne was still in labour and the potential for something to go wrong still existed.

He was also held here by the obscure notion that the emotional punishment this represented was deserved because he'd thought so badly of Anne. He'd thought she could have fallen into the arms of another man within weeks of his departure. Even—in the wakeful hours of a particularly dark night—that the whole disintegration of their relationship had been engineered as a way of escape because there had already been someone else in the wings.

He'd almost convinced himself that Anne had arranged to have all those dates or times together interrupted by urgent calls so that he'd never seemed to be a priority in her life. That she'd discovered what he wanted most in life—a future with her that included a family—and had simply taken half of that equation away from him.

No negotiation but compromise wasn't in Anne Bennett's vocabulary, was it? He stood there now, as Emily waited to catch the second twin, and saw the lines of effort and pain contort Anne's face as she pushed.

What an extraordinary thing to be doing for someone else. Months of discomfort and change. Physical risk. Pain.

It was typical of the woman he knew, though, wasn't it? She was such a black-and-white person. All or nothing. If she had decided to help her sister because she couldn't have her own baby, then she would have gone all the way.

Anne was gasping now, between contractions, clearly very tired. Mac had his hands on her shoulders, trying to encourage her to slow her breathing.

'In, one...two...three... Out, one...two... three...'

Julia was still holding the baby boy, now wrapped in a warm cover but her gaze was fixed on her sister.

'You're doing great, Annie. I love you...'

'Another push should do it,' Emily said. 'Wait for the next contraction and give it all you've got, Anne.'

David found himself holding his breath, as caught up in this as everybody present was. Along with some excited staff on the other side of the curtain, eager for news. Successful birth stories were actually quite unusual in an emergency department and this was no ordinary story. It had captured imaginations.

Anne would be considered a heroine doing this for her sister.

His thoughts circled back to what he knew of her personality. So black and white. She wanted her career and was, therefore, not going to have children of her own. She had wanted the experience of childbirth but not to be a parent.

Heroic? Or...selfish?

Lord, where had that come from? Some pocket of envy because Anne was prepared to do this for someone other than himself? He knew it was unfair. He knew that what he was seeing here was total commitment. The positive side of being black and white.

He'd experienced that commitment himself. Maybe that was why the thought of Anne being with anyone else had been such a shock. She didn't do half-measures. She did total commitment and he'd had it in their relationship. He'd known that every time he'd touched her. When she allowed herself to succumb to passion she had given everything she had to give.

Demanded all from him.

An explosive mix that had always left them completely satisfied. Drained so that the cares of the world trickled away. Content to the point of utter bliss.

Nobody else had ever given him that. Or demanded it from him. Not that he'd want to give that much of himself to anyone else. He couldn't. He'd already given it away.

To Anne.

The second baby was emerging now. A girl who looked to be pretty much the same size as her brother. Small but not enough to need special care. She was crying already, sounding healthy.

The beds were manoeuvred so that this baby could lie on Julia's stomach cradled by one of each of her parents' hands as they waited for the cord to stop pulsing before it was cut. For a minute, they were all joined. The babies, their biological parents and their birth mother.

An incredible family unit. No wonder there were smiles and tears amongst the soft words being spoken as the babies were introduced to each other and the world. Angus was going to be the boy's name. The girl was Amy.

When Mac cut the cord of the second baby, Anne could have sworn she felt it herself.

It had been weird lying here, still connected to the tiny girl who was lying on Julia's stomach. She could see the miracle of this gift in her sister's face. The wonder and the joy of it. And she could see—and feel—overwhelming love. Between Julia and Mac and between these new parents and their babies. A solid force that she was part of but separate from.

And then the cord was cut and she felt the separation increase.

Almost desperately, she scanned what she could see of the twins. Imprinting the memory of their bare skin and crinkled little faces. All those fingers and toes that Mac and Julia were touching in reverence. She wanted to touch them herself.

To count them, as all new parents did.

She wanted to hold them and have those

serious dark eyes calmly watching *her* the way these babies, now quiet, were watching Julia. Imprinting their mother's face on their brains the way she was with them.

Her breasts ached. Anne was barely aware of what Emily was doing at the end of the bed. The calm voice telling her that the placentas seemed fine and that she hadn't torn at all and wasn't it great that she wouldn't need a single stitch? She was too distracted by pulling advice from her head. The words of the counsellor that had seemed so sensible to all involved at the time.

Don't breastfeed, even once, no matter how strong the urge might be. It's a mistake physically because it will stimulate milk supply and make the drying-up process a lot harder. It will also create an emotional connection that could have repercussions none of you will want.

They had all been so clear about what they wanted. Anne would love and cherish these babies, of course, but she wasn't their mother. Julia was. She'd been a human incubator but she was only their aunt. A very special aunt, certainly, but she had to be one step removed. She had to allow Julia and Mac to parent these children without interference or pressure of any kind. For the next few weeks, in fact, she was going to have nothing more than minimal contact while the new family bonded.

She needed time to recover from the ordeal her body had been through. So many changes with the grand finale of birth. The power of those changes had been a revelation to Anne and it was helpful to remember that. This desperate urge to hold the babies and feed them was probably nothing more than a fresh burst of hormonal activity.

Astonishingly powerful, these hormones. It was incredibly hard not to reach out her hand. Almost impossible to drag her gaze away from the infants. And when she did, she found David watching her with an oddly intense expression.

Or maybe it wasn't so odd. It hadn't been that long ago that they'd been deeply in love and so in tune with each other they could pick up on thoughts and emotions in a kind of telepathy.

Was he picking up what she was thinking now? Would he interpret her desire to hold these babies as an admission that she'd been wrong all along? That she just hadn't known how much she did want children of her own?

She *didn't*. She hadn't been wrong. Oh, no. She had to escape David's gaze. It was making her feel confused. Maybe she *had* been wrong.

Anne closed her eyes, which made it much easier to think straight. No. It was still there. The conviction that she wasn't wrong. She'd given up too much of what she wanted in life already. Her childhood, to become a mother to the baby sister she'd adored. Her social life as a teenager and medical student. Sports and hobbies and anything else that took up too much time or money. Things had always been put on hold. She had always promised herself that she could have her life on her own terms once Julia didn't need her any more.

That time was now.

Julia had Mac. They had their babies. This moment was more than the birth of a family.

It was the birth of her own future as well. Life without sacrifice for someone else. Was that selfish?

Maybe, but she deserved it, didn't she? After everything she'd given up? Everything she'd been through for the person she loved the most?

But she had loved David too. Still did, even though she didn't dare admit how much.

This was so hard. So confusing. Anne opened her eyes to find that David was now looking at the bed beside her. Somehow, Mac had made room to get onto the bed and cradle Julia in his arms and her arms were full of babies. Two dark little heads, one in the crook of each elbow. They seemed to be asleep now. Mac's head was tilted and Julia's forehead rested against his cheek. They were both looking down at the babies and someone, bless them, had produced a camera and was taking the first family photos.

David didn't seem to be as entranced by the photo shoot as everyone else. When her own gaze shifted she found him looking at her again. No worries about telepathy now. He looked distant. Cold, even.

As though it was sinking in that she'd given her sister something she was never willing to give him.

How could she be like this?

To give birth and not want to hold the babies? Fair enough that she didn't want to breastfeed but to not even touch them?

Cutting that second umbilical cord had seemed to sever Anne's involvement. Her sister and her brother-in-law and the babies were a unit. On a separate bed. Might as well have been on a separate planet.

How ironic that he should have been present to witness Anne deliver babies that she had no desire to parent in any way. Fate was handing him a graphic illustration of everything that had gone wrong with their relationship, really. There wasn't any point in him being in here any longer. Emily was in charge.

'We'll get you up to Maternity,' she was telling

Julia. 'I think we'll keep you all in overnight. The babies are a reasonable weight but I want a full paediatric check on them both and we want to make sure they're feeding well.'

The consultant turned back to Anne then. Oddly, David got the impression that there was sympathy in her smile and gentle tone. 'I'd like to keep you in overnight, too, Anne. In another ward, maybe?'

David sucked in a breath. Had they already discussed these arrangements? Emily seemed aware that Anne wanted as little contact with the babies as possible. She was shaking her head.

'I don't want to stay.'

'Do you have anyone at home?'

'No.'

The thought of her going home alone after an experience like this was too sad for words but David strangled the desire to offer comfort or support. She'd chosen this path. She didn't have to be alone. She wanted to be.

'It was a normal delivery,' Anne said wearily.

'And I feel fine. What's the minimum time you keep women in these days?'

'We let mothers go home after six hours if they choose but…they're not usually by themselves.'

'I've got a phone. I'll call for help if I need it.'

'I could come home with you, Annie,' Mac offered.

David could feel a muscle in his jaw begin to ache from tension but again Anne shook her head.

'You stay with Jules. With your family. They need you.'

Julia was chewing her bottom lip. 'This is wrong,' she said with a wobble in her voice. 'We need *you*, too, Annie. We want to look after you.'

David could see the shine of tears in Anne's eyes. So she wasn't being as hard hearted as he thought. Again, he had to fight an urge to step closer.

'I know, hon,' she said to Julia. 'But I'll be fine, honestly. We made a plan, remember?'

Julia nodded, dislodging unshed tears. 'But...'

'I'll visit tomorrow.'

They were getting ready to start moving the bed. Mac climbed off. Julia turned her head so that she could still see Anne. 'Call me?'

'I will. First thing in the morning when I'm home.'

David found Emily by his side. 'Perhaps Anne could stay down here for observation?'

'Sure.' He would be going home soon enough. As Anne had said herself, the delivery had been uncomplicated. Any registrar could monitor her condition until she was discharged in a few hours. He didn't have to go anywhere near her.

Except he couldn't stay away.

An hour later her found Anne asleep in the side room but with a second check in another hour or so, he found her awake.

'How are you feeling?'

'Kind of like I've been run over by a bus.'

'I'm not surprised.' David stood at the end of her bed. The silence grew and became awkward. There was so much he could have said. Wanted to say. Impossible to know how to start. He needed to apologise but there was a barrier there created by hurt. He wanted to ask why but was so sure he wouldn't like the answer that even that tiny word stuck in his throat.

Finally, he picked up the observation chart. 'Your blood pressure's fine,' he told her. 'Everything's looking good.'

'I could go home then.' Her voice was flat.

'Soon. I…guess you'll be taking some time off?'

Anne gave a small huff of sound. 'Three months. I was due a sabbatical but the first few weeks were supposed to be resting in late pregnancy.'

'You'll still need to rest and recuperate.'

'That was the plan for the second month. Then I'm negotiating to spend a month in an overseas unit that specialises in paediatric chest trauma.'

'Oh...' David had a three-month locum. By the time Anne returned for work, he'd be gone.

It should be a relief.

'Maybe I can bring it forward,' Anne said.

Which would take her out of the country. He wouldn't see her again. Possibly ever.

'Maybe we could...meet up before you go,' he heard himself saying aloud. 'We haven't had much of a chance to...talk or anything.'

'No.' Another tiny huff at the understatement. Anne closed her eyes again but not before he'd seen a flash of agreement. Even...what, *hope*?

'I'm really tired right now,' she said.

'I'll leave you to rest, then.' He couldn't push her, however much he'd like to find out what she'd been thinking before she'd closed her eyes. She had to be totally exhausted, both physically and emotionally. He understood that. He knew this wasn't the time to talk but David still hesitated. Opened his mouth to say something else.

As though sensing his intention, Anne turned

her head to face away from him. There was nothing for it but to respect the dismissal and leave.

Anne kept her eyes tightly closed.

She wanted to talk to David. Of course she did. He deserved an explanation. An apology even, but she couldn't find the words right now. Not while she was feeling like this. As though she had lost something infinitely precious.

Something she would never be able to find again.

It didn't seem to matter how tightly she kept her eyes squeezed shut.

Her tears still managed to escape.

CHAPTER FOUR

SHE couldn't stop thinking about him.

The way he'd looked, standing at the end of her bed the other night. The light may have been subdued but there had been no mistaking the look of pain on his features.

She'd seen that look before. More than once in those difficult, final weeks of their relationship, when the distance between them had become an unbridgeable gulf. The unspoken messages were so eloquent.

I don't want this.

It's unbearable.

Why has it come to this?

How did it all go so terribly wrong?

Can we fix it?

No...

The lines etched on David's face may have

been personal but his body language and actions had been nothing but professional. The way he'd stood with the length of the bed between them. The way he'd reached to pick up her chart instead of touching *her*.

'Everything's looking good,' he'd said.

Couldn't he see that she was desperately unhappy? That it was beginning to seem like a huge mistake, being a human incubator for someone else? It had become such a huge part of her life, being so intimately connected to the two tiny beings growing inside her.

She would never forget feeling those first movements. So subtle they had felt like nothing more than a stream of tiny bubbles. Being so aware of the strength increasing as the weeks went on. Strong movements then, that had often startled her. An uncomfortable prod from an elbow or a kick that could make the skin on her stomach bulge and make her laugh in a mixture of amazement and amusement.

And the hiccups that had felt like a clock ticking inside her. The soft flutters that could only be felt from deep within and she would imagine her babies sleeping. A leg brushing against another limb perhaps or a reach to hold hands as she'd seen ultrasound pictures of twins doing in the womb.

Whoa! *Her* babies?

Anne sighed deeply and dragged herself up from the armchair she'd been sitting in for hours now. A still unopened medical journal slid from her lap to the floor.

That was the problem in a nutshell, wasn't it? They had never been *her* babies. Julia's eggs. Mac's sperm. Yes, she'd had custody of the precious little lives for eight months but they'd never been *hers*. She'd known that all along. She'd thought she was more than prepared for how it would feel to hand them over. She'd never for a moment expected it to feel as though something was being ripped away from her soul.

For it to have been *so* hard.

Tears were slipping down her face and she scrubbed at them angrily. What had Jules said that day? That she never cried. Well, she'd made up for it in the last few days, that's for sure, and today was the worst yet. She was like a tap in dire need of a plumber's attention today.

So many sad thoughts that she couldn't shake off. Of babies she ached to hold. Of David's face as he'd stood there at the end of her bed. Of how much she'd missed him over the last year and of how unbridgeable that gap between them was. Especially now.

How ironic that he should have been there when the babies were born.

How unfair!

Intending to go into the kitchen to make a cup of tea, Anne had to pause before she got more than a step or two. She had to reach out and grasp the back of the armchair as a wave of dizziness threatened to make her knees buckle.

Oh...*God*!

Blindly, thanks to a fresh spurt of tears, she felt her way back to a sitting position and then buried her face in her hands with a groan of despair.

What was wrong with her? She was a doctor, for heaven's sake. She should be able to figure out what was happening here and then do something about it.

What was the main problem?

Her breasts hurt. They were as hard as rocks and aching so much she couldn't bear to wear a bra despite knowing that the support might help. She had taken some anti-inflammatories and had tried an ice-pack earlier today but neither remedy had helped much. Maybe she should try that old wives' treatment of cabbage leaves or something. Another dose of drugs, anyway.

What else? She felt hot, which could be because her armchair was in front of a window in direct sunlight she hadn't been aware of. She also felt faintly nauseated but when had she last had something to eat? It was probably lunchtime by now. A glance at her watch startled her. It was well into the afternoon. Where had all those hours gone? Hard to feel hungry when her belly hurt as though she was in the middle of a particularly heavy period. This amount of discomfort had also been unexpected but her postnatal bleeding hadn't been heavy enough to be a concern.

The main problem was something that was simply making everything else seem worse. The fact that she was alone. That it was day three after giving birth and, while she might have been prepared for the so called 'baby blues', she hadn't realised how hard it would be to deal with them alone.

She could ring Julia but she'd probably burst into tears on the phone and that would worry her sister. What if she heard the babies crying in the background and was unable to get any words out at all? Julia would dispatch Mac to find out what was wrong and he would probably insist on staying or taking her home with him so that she could have company and be looked after.

And that wasn't part of the plan they had stuck to so well so far.

She had gone to visit after her discharge from the emergency department. She had been able to admire the sleeping infants and be as delighted as Julia and Mac that the feeding was going well and they would all be able to go home later that day. She hadn't touched the babies because she needed to create some distance. Not for ever. Just for as long as it took for her hormones to settle down a bit.

And that was all this was all about. Baby blues. Hormones. It was a form of depression and the best treatment was distraction. Physical exercise.

Pleased with her clinical assessment, Anne tried to stand up again. This time her head felt fine. She'd just been sitting still for too long. She hadn't been eating enough. What she needed to do was get a grip and ride this out and in a day or two she would be feeling much better. What on earth had she been thinking, letting herself just sit around latching onto sad things to dwell on?

She had so much to look forward to, didn't she? Being an aunt to the two most beautiful babies in the universe. Time away from work to do something that she would love—like spending time in a clinical facility that was achieving results she admired tremendously. And right now she could go out and enjoy this gorgeous day. It wasn't too late to feel the warmth of sun on her skin. To get a bit of fresh air and escape four walls that were closing both her body and mind into an unfamiliar, and very unwelcome, prison.

Good call, she congratulated herself a short time later. She felt better already, even if the bright light was hurting eyes that had been bathed in far too much salty fluid today.

Planning a route for this gentle walk was too hard. Her brain was crying out for a rest. An escape from sad thoughts and decision-making. With a sigh of relief, Anne surrendered to just following her feet, content to enjoy the warmth and the colours in the pockets of the inner-city gardens she passed. For the first time in her life, she actually had the chance to stop and smell the roses.

That had to be another good thing, surely?

He couldn't stop thinking about her.

The way she'd been lying, alone on that hospital bed, radiating unhappiness.

He'd been contributing to that misery, hadn't he? The feeling of distance between them was all too familiar. He'd pushed and pushed to try and get what he'd wanted in the past and all he'd achieved had been to push her so far away he'd lost her.

With an outward breath verging on a sigh, David tapped a finger on the X-ray image on the screen.

'Right there, see? Probably a stress fracture. Not major but it'll be causing the pain. She needs to go to the bone shop and get a cast on.'

'She won't be happy. She's training for a tri-athalon.'

David grimaced, unconsciously rolling his head to try and ease the ache between his shoulder blades. 'Try telling her that exercise is over-rated.'

His junior colleague grinned. 'You still suffering, then?'

'I think it's getting worse. I'm seizing up.'

'Keep moving, then,' the registrar advised

cheekily, trying to stifle his amusement. 'It's the best cure for soft-tissue injuries.'

'No. The best cure is prevention.' David straightened his back with a groan. 'Which is why I'm going to find a landscaping firm to come and tame that jungle that used to be my garden. Know anyone with a bulldozer?'

'Talk to Di on the front desk. I think her son is some kind of gardener.'

'I'll do that. Thanks. Was there anything else you needed to talk to me about?'

'No. Sorry to hold you up. It's past home time for you, isn't it?'

'Sure is.' David took a final glance around the department. He eyed a telephone on the triage desk and once again the thought of Anne crossed his mind.

It wouldn't hurt to call, would it? Just to see how she was doing?

No. He turned towards the reception area instead, intent on tracking down the woman who might have an expert gardener for a son. Anne wouldn't want to talk to him. Not yet, anyway. In a week or two, maybe, when she had recovered a bit more from the birth.

The desire to talk to her was getting stronger every day, along with a faint hope that they could possibly salvage some kind of friendship from the ruins of the relationship they'd had. One that would give him a new base from which to move forward. One that wasn't built on anger and hurt and loss.

He could afford to wait. His two days off had made him realise what an enormous job it was going to be trying to get his property in shape to do well on the market. The garden was impenetrable in places and while he'd actually enjoyed wielding a pickaxe and clippers, despite the after-effects on his body, he hadn't made much progress.

And the garden was only part of what needed to be done. Trying to distract himself from thinking about Anne when he wasn't sweating outside had led him to wandering around the big house, cataloging tasks that needed attention inside. Plumbing needed work. There was dry rot in some of the windowsills. The paint and wallpaper were tired to the point of being shabby but if they were improved the carpets and curtains would look infinitely worse. He needed a team of interior decorators as well as some landscaping experts.

Maybe Di would have some more useful contacts.

Twenty minutes later, David emerged into the late afternoon sunshine, armed with a host of suggestions and phone numbers gleaned from the *Yellow Pages* and Di's advice. Feeling far more positive, he decided to leave his car in the parking building and walk home. That registrar was quite right. Keeping his sore muscles moving was the best thing he could do for them.

It was a pleasant walk. The small river that wound through the central city had wide grassed banks and huge, ancient chestnut trees dotted at regular intervals. Park benches had been sited beneath many of the trees and there were a lot of people out enjoying the late afternoon warmth. A man reading a newspaper. A couple with young children who were feeding stale crusts to an expanding group of enthusiastic ducks. A woman, sitting alone with her head drooping, as though she was being lulled to sleep by the peaceful surroundings.

Something made David take another look at the lone woman as he came closer. And his heart missed a beat.

'Anne.'

She looked dreadful. As white as a sheet, and she seemed to be shivering despite the warmth of the day. She also seemed to be having trouble focusing on his face. Or maybe she didn't want to look at him. She was looking down again now, her eyes drifting shut. He couldn't walk away, however. No way.

'What are you doing here?'

'I...I came out for a walk.' Good grief, were her words a little slurred? 'Such a nice day...'

'But you're a long way from home. You're almost at the hospital.'

'Am I?' She looked up and blinked in bewilderment. 'I hadn't noticed.'

'Anne…' David crouched in front of her and touched her knee. 'Are you all right?'

She was looking at him now, her eyes wide. Startled, almost.

'No,' she whispered. 'I don't think I am.'

David swallowed. Hard. 'What's happening?'

Anne drew in a long, shaky breath. 'Things hurt,' she admitted.

'What things?'

'Um…my tummy.' The huff of laughter was pure embarrassment. 'My…ah…boobs.'

David couldn't help the quirk of his lips but it was a poignant twist. If he'd needed any indication that Anne was not herself right now, this total lack of medical terminology did the trick.

'Anything else?'

Anne nodded but said nothing. David waited, holding the eye contact. Encouraging her to tell him what was going on. She didn't look away. She was hanging onto his gaze as though it was a lifeline, in fact.

'What else, Annie?' he prompted gently.

'I...I've *missed* you,' Anne said. And burst into tears.

Oh...Lord! What could he do but ease himself onto the bench beside her and take her into his arms? Hold her until the sobs—that were as uncharacteristic as her layman's anatomy—finally dwindled into a kind of ripple he could feel but no longer hear. And he had to try very hard not to put any undue significance on the words she had just uttered. She had *missed* him? As much as he'd missed her? Enough to make compromise an acceptable alternative?

'Sorry,' Anne muttered. 'Oh, I'm sorry, David.'

'It's okay. It's fine.' He didn't want her to be sorry because it might mean she wanted to take back what she'd said.

'No. No, it's not. I'm...' Anne was pushing at him. He had to fight the urge to tighten his hold. He had to let her go.

'I'm *so* sorry.' She was scrubbing at her face. 'I don't know what's wrong with me.'

'You've got a lot going on. Mentally and physically.' She wasn't herself. He had to remember that. She'd said she'd missed him like she'd meant it but she wasn't herself so it didn't mean anything. 'You're not…well.'

'I'm not sick.' Anne gave her head a shake. 'Childbirth is a natural process, not some kind of disease.' She gave her face a final wipe, pushing her hair back and then holding it in a ponytail with one hand behind her neck. It made her look much more in control.

'I'm fine, really,' she said as she stood up.

David watched her. He could almost see the way the strength it had taken to stand up ebbed from her body. The way her eyes, made so much darker by her pale face, seemed to glaze over. He was on his feet by the time she began to sway. He had scooped her into his arms by the time she lost consciousness.

Ignoring the horrified stares of people on the riverbank, he strode back towards the emergency department of the hospital. He was barely aware of the weight in his arms and it certainly didn't slow his pace.

* * *

She was waking up from the deepest sleep.

Or maybe she was still dreaming. She could feel the strength of a man's arms around her and feel the warmth of his skin close to her face. Anne's eyes flickered open. It was his neck. Her head was cradled on his shoulder and he had one arm around her back and the other under her knees.

Her bones had melted away. She had never been this relaxed. So secure she didn't want to move in case she broke the spell. The ground was moving fast beneath them and it made her feel sick so she closed her eyes again, rolling her head a little so that her mouth and nose were even closer to that skin.

She could even imagine she recognised the smell of this man. That the arms around her were David's. That he was carrying her somewhere safe where nothing could hurt any more and she would never feel lonely ever again.

The rocking continued. Even more comforting was the murmur of his voice, telling her she was going to be fine. That she would be looked after.

That *he* would look after her because he cared. He'd missed her *so* much. The words weren't all that clear, maybe, but she could understand them perfectly.

But the movement changed and became jerky. The words became clearer.

'Complained of abdominal pain…'

'Gave birth three days ago. Twins.'

A new voice then. 'She's lost a fair amount of blood.'

The security of those arms was loosening. Anne felt herself being tipped. Put down on something firm and cool. Felt the softness of a pillow next to her face. The loss of those arms was enough to make her groan in distress.

'You're all right, Anne. You're in the emergency department now.'

'W-what?' She forced her eyes open and blinked, trying to focus on the face close to hers. 'What happened?'

'You've had a bit of a postnatal bleed. You fainted, down by the river. You don't remember?'

'I...' How much had been reality and how much a dream? Had David really been telling her how much he'd missed her? How much he still cared? It would be safer to assume that those impressions had been the workings of an unconscious mind. 'No,' she said softly. 'I don't remember much of anything.'

Surely that wasn't disappointment she could see in his eyes? She tried to hang onto the contact so she could interpret the fleeting expression properly but David was standing up now. And the sharp pain in her arm was distracting.

'Ouch!'

'Try and keep still.' David had a hand on her arm. 'We're just getting IV access. Your blood pressure's well down and you need some fluids. Possibly a transfusion.'

She heard orders being given. For blood tests that needed to be done. For an urgent call for an ultrasound technician. The blood-pressure cuff she hadn't been aware of tightened on her other arm. Someone was hanging a bag of saline overhead. An oxygen mask was being slipped onto her face and someone was peeling away her clothing.

Anne shut her eyes. This no longer bore any resemblance to a dream. It was far more like a nightmare.

Except that David was still here. Looking after her. He didn't have to be because Anne had heard someone sounding very surprised that he was here at all because his shift had finished ages ago.

'I'm staying,' he told whoever it was. 'Anne and I go back a long way. We're…friends.'

Friends?

Were they?

It didn't feel true but it would be nice if it was. Friends cared about each other and made life less lonely. Anne didn't have many close friends. She had her work and colleagues and she had her family and…not much else.

Fighting a strong need to sleep, Anne pushed her eyelids open, hoping to find David amongst the people crowding around her bed. A technician was squeezing gel onto her stomach.

'Sorry, this is a bit cold.'

Anne ignored the apology, looking from one person to the next. If David was there, she could smile at him, maybe, to let him know that she liked what he'd said. That she wanted the statement about being friends to be the truth.

But she couldn't see him anywhere.

He could have been home again by now.

Why on earth had he said he'd stay? That he and Anne were friends. An unfortunate distortion of the truth…or wishful thinking?

David was pacing back and forth in his office. He'd said he would stay but that didn't mean he had to be in the room with her the whole time, did it? She was safe. The doctors on duty were taking good care of her and treatment was under way. He could go and check up on how she was doing and then go home.

He wanted to leave.

He wanted to stay.

No. What he really wanted was to be in that

room with Anne. Beside the bed. Holding her hand.

How stupid would it be to get sucked even further into what was going on in her life?

It wasn't going to happen.

So what if the attraction was still there? That it had hit him like a brick that moment he'd first seen her again, looking so rounded and luscious and glowing with her pregnancy. There had been nothing sexual about the way he'd held her as she'd cried today but it had revealed something a lot deeper. That he still cared. A lot. Too much. Carrying her towards medical help like that, not knowing what was wrong or how serious it might be, had smashed through more than one of those defensive barriers he'd carefully constructed. Or maybe that first wall had fallen when she'd said she had missed him.

With a sound rather like a growl of frustration, David circled his office again, ramming his fingers through his hair as he tried to think through the turbulent mix of emotions tearing him apart.

There was absolutely no point in this agonising and he'd done far too much of it already. He knew the way forward, he just had to pull himself together. He could deal with this. The whole purpose of coming back here had been to tie up loose ends. The end of his relationship might have seemed like a tight knot but it had completely unravelled in the last week. There were loose ends all over the place, snapping at him like tiny emotional whips.

David left the office only a minute or so later. Much calmer.

In control.

He would check up on Anne's condition—as any friend would. He would offer support if she needed it because there was very little danger of her accepting, and then he could escape. Never mind that daylight was fading fast. He would go home, ignore his aching muscles, and find something that needed doing with a pickaxe in his garden.

* * *

The feeling of safety that being carried here in David's arms had engendered was long gone.

Anne was in a side room now, with the kind of privacy a consultant automatically received if it was available. A privileged space that should have been a peaceful refuge from the bustle of the emergency department.

But there were two tiny babies cocooned in their car seats on the floor beside Anne's bed and they were both whimpering. Their mother wasn't any happier.

'I still can't believe you didn't call when you were feeling so lousy. My God, Annie…'

'Don't fuss, Jules. I'm all right.'

'You might not have been. We should never have let you go home by yourself. The plan was stupid.'

'No.' Anne shook her head wearily. The whimpering of the babies was increasing in strength and the sound felt like a chainsaw inside her head. 'I was doing fine.'

'Are you kidding? Mac's at your house right

now, collecting the stuff you'll need. You left the stove on, Annie. *And* the tap.'

Anne winced. Again. 'I know. I'd been planning to make some lunch before I went for a walk. I…must have got distracted, that's all, and forgot I'd turned anything on.'

'You're lucky the house just flooded and didn't burn to the ground with you lying unconscious on the floor.' Julia was shaking her head in consternation but then her chin jerked up. 'David!'

'Is that true?' came the familiar voice from the doorway. 'Anne flooded her house?'

'Tried to burn it down as well. It's my fault. I should never have agreed to let her go home by herself.'

David was staring down at the babies. 'Are they hungry?'

'I'll feed them in a minute. I had to come and see Anne first. We just threw everything and everyone in the car when they rang to say Anne was in here. Someone found her down by the river, would you believe? Carried her here, unconscious.'

'Mmm.' David's glance towards Anne held a sparkle of amusement. 'I would believe it. It was me that carried her.'

'Oh…' Julia's jaw dropped and she dragged her gaze from David back to Anne. 'You didn't tell me that.'

'You haven't given me a chance to say much at all.'

Julia ignored the implied reprimand. 'Mac's gone to collect Annie's stuff,' she informed David. 'We'll be taking her home with us.'

'No.' Anne managed to find the strength to sound decisive. 'I'm not going home with you, Jules.'

'But you *have* to.'

'No, I don't.' The babies were howling now. Anne closed her eyes in a desperate attempt to shut out her surroundings, but not before she caught sight of a nurse entering the room, closely followed by Mac who was carrying a suitcase.

'Dr Bennett really needs some peace and quiet to rest,' the nurse told Julia.

Mac looked at David and then at Anne. He put

the suitcase down and picked up a handle of a car seat in each hand. 'Come on,' he ordered his wife. 'Let's go and deal with these two. We can come back when they're quiet enough not to be upsetting anybody.'

The nurse nodded her approval. 'I'll take you to the relatives' room.' She closed the door behind the noisy procession.

Anne cautiously opened her eyes. David was still here.

'How are you doing?' he asked.

She gave a tiny huff of sound. 'Better now, thanks.'

David glanced at the door as though still seeing the babies being taken away. His face was expressionless as he turned back.

'I hear the final verdict was a patch of retained placenta.'

Anne nodded. 'Probably a succinturiate lobe that didn't get missed at the time, being an extra bit. Hardly surprising when they had two to check in somewhat unusual circumstances.'

David ignored the reference to her surrogacy. 'But you're not up for a D&C?'

'No.' Anne's sigh of relief was heartfelt. 'Not that they'd do one immediately anyway, with the uterus being so friable, but Emily thinks that bleed I had when I fainted must have cleared the last of it. Going by the ultrasound, it's all good.'

'Infection? You looked a bit feverish.'

'Yeah, I've been cooking a few bugs. Nothing that the antibiotics I'm on now won't fix.'

'And your haemoglobin?'

'Down a bit but not enough to warrant a transfusion, thank heavens. I'll be a bit wobbly for a day or two, that's all.'

'So you'll go and stay with your sister?'

Anne shook her head slowly. 'I'd prefer not to.'

'Why?' The word was crisp. Cool, even. 'Because you'd rather not see the babies?'

Anne bit her lip to stop the prickle of tears. She couldn't expect him to understand, so why did it hurt so much? She might have won the battle with the tears but she couldn't help the tremor in her voice.

'It's more that I want to see them *too* much.'

David's face went very still. It was impossible not to let her gaze rest on him. Tracing lines she knew so well while she tried to gauge whether he was prepared to try and understand. Those tiny crinkles at the corners of his eyes. The deep furrows that joined his nose to the corners of his mouth that would deepen when he smiled. Not that he was smiling right now. He seemed to be returning her gaze with equal intensity.

'They're not my babies,' she explained softly. 'Not even part of them. Jules had her eggs collected and Mac's sperm fertilised them. I had the embryos implanted. My head knows perfectly well that they're not *my* babies but…but my body's not quite singing from the same hymn book yet.' Her smile was even more precarious than her voice. 'I'm a bit of a mess emotionally, to tell you the truth.'

An eyebrow quirked on David's forehead. 'Really? Can't say I noticed.'

His smile was as gentle as his humour. It was the kind of smile that Anne hadn't seen since way back…way before things had begun to fall apart. It touched something deep inside her. Something that brought tears to her eyes that were even harder to control this time.

She blinked. Hard.'I'll be fine,' she said with a good attempt at bravado. 'In fact, I think the worst is over now. I probably didn't realise how much it was all due to this complication. Being sick on top of everything else. I'll bounce back in no time now.'

'But you can't go home by yourself.'

'No. She can't.' Mac, with a sleeping infant in his arms, had come quietly into the room.

David saw something like fear flare in Anne's eyes. Did she think that Mac might have overheard what she'd been saying? It was obvious she didn't want her sister or Mac to know how difficult she was finding this situation. She was still protecting her baby sister, wasn't she? Prepared to go through hell herself. By herself.

He almost groaned aloud as he felt himself getting entangled a little further in that complicated web of emotion, past and present. There was respect. And caring. And…a moral duty, perhaps.

'I could stay here overnight, I suppose,' Anne said. 'If things don't get too busy. I'll have to go home in the morning anyway and sort out what needs to be done to sort out the mess.'

'I'll take care of that,' Mac said. 'I'll get hold of your insurance company. They can send their assessors and they'll know what needs to be done to dry things out and what will have to be replaced.'

Anne looked like she was trying hard not to cry. Seeing the damage to her home and belongings was the last thing she needed when she was, by her own admission, an emotional basket case.

Julia had come into the room again now and she was holding a baby in her arms that was as quiet as the one Mac was holding. She stood beside her husband. Had the babies been fed and changed already or had they only needed a cuddle from their parents to settle? Not that it mattered. They were content and their parents stood close enough for their bodies to touch. They were the picture of the perfect family and suddenly David could see that picture through Anne's eyes. Could see the babies she had given birth to but had to distance herself from.

How much harder would it be to have to stay in the same house?

'I have an idea,' he heard himself saying aloud. His words held the confidence of a brainwave and it was no surprise to find three sets of adult eyes focusing on him. He couldn't not say it now.

'Anne could come home with me.'

CHAPTER FIVE

GOOD grief!

Had David really said that?

Anne stared at him, her lips parted but there were no words available to emerge. Her brain felt fuzzy. Short-circuited in some way by that simple statement.

Come home with me

Could it be that simple? Did he want her back? Enough to compromise the dreams he'd had for the future? How good would that be, to have David in her life again? And her career uninterrupted. And a little nephew and niece to include in their world. It was going to be enough for her to have that extended family. Maybe it could be enough for David, too?

No. Of course it couldn't. The stupid, romantic

fantasy was just an indication of what a basket case she was at the moment.

'No,' she said aloud into the stunned silence.

Julia was biting her lip. She looked up at Mac.

'It's a big house,' David added. 'And I'm working pretty long hours. I'd be around but she probably wouldn't even see that·much of me.'

'She' ? They were talking about her as if she wasn't there. Mac was actually nodding at what David had said. 'Be more peaceful than our place,' he said. 'And it *would* only be for a few days.'

Anne tried very hard to keep any tremor out of her voice. 'So I'd be by myself in a big house. And that would be better for me how? I could go to a hotel. I'd have plenty of peace and quiet that way. Room service as well.'

'You wouldn't be alone at my place,' David said.

He said it so calmly. As though she shouldn't be surprised. But she was. More than surprised. She was shocked. David was sharing his house with someone. Another woman? Entirely plausible. It had been more than a year after all. How many men went that long without finding a companion? Especially when they were pushing forty and they'd made no secret about their need to find a life partner that shared their dreams.

David was still talking. With an effort, Anne tuned back in.

'...coming and going all day. The guest suite is private enough but there would certainly be company, or assistance, if it was required.'

Anne tried to fish missing clues from her head. Words that had floated past without being listened to while she dealt with that shock. He'd mentioned builders. Decorators. Gardeners perhaps?

Yes. He was talking about a restoration job on his property. Contractors. Julia didn't seem to be listening any more than Anne had been. She was looking at her sister and as Anne met her gaze, she was drawn into the close connection they had always had. The ability to communicate without words so easily. And this was such a familiar pattern of reassurance. Julia was worried. More than that. In that glance, Anne realised she hadn't been hiding her confusion about the babies as well as she'd thought. There was an awful lot riding on how she handled this.

I understand, she signalled silently with a tiny smile. *But everything's going to work out just fine, you'll see.*

'What do you think, Annie?' Mac was looking just as anxious as Julia.

'No,' she said again. The word lacked the conviction of her earlier refusal, however. She was trying to think of an alternative.

David was looking uncomfortable. Maybe he was regretting his offer? 'Do you have any other friends you could land on at short notice?' he asked.

'No.' A quiet word this time. Was David implying that he could be a friend? A *friend*? How could it sound like such a small, insignificant thing when only an hour or two ago she'd been trying to catch his gaze? To smile at him and let him know that she approved of him describing her as nothing more than that.

This was really rock bottom, wasn't it? Here she was, virtually incapacitated and faced with two choices that were equally undesirable for very different reasons. Both of them were emotional minefields.

Another glance at Julia finally made the decision simple. Neither choice would be great for herself but one would definitely be much better for her baby sister. She couldn't stay here using up a bed in a busy emergency department when she didn't need to. Nobody in this room was going to allow her an independent choice like a hotel and she was too tired to fight. It would only be for a day or two after all. A mere blink in a lifetime.

'David's house is a lot closer to mine,' she said. 'It would certainly make it easier to supervise getting my place sorted.'

'And you'd be doing me a favour,' David nodded. 'For the same reason. I've only got a limited time frame to get the work done on my house. Having someone they think might be looking over their shoulders occasionally would keep the workmen on track.'

There. It was settled. Anne managed to smile. Now that the decision was made she had a goal. All she had to do was focus and get her home and then her life back in order. Knowledge was power. Strength. She could do this.

'I'd like a quick cuddle with those babies, please,' she said calmly. 'And then you'd better get them home.'

'Before they start howling again, you mean?' Mac's tone was gentle as he stepped forward to place one of the neatly wrapped bundles in Anne's arms.

'Exactly. One of the many benefits in being an aunty.'

The guest suite was next to the garage complex but the bedroom had a pretty bay window that would have a lovely outlook into the garden in the daylight. It also had a small sitting room with a desk and couch and, thankfully, it had its own bathroom. No need to risk running into David elsewhere in the house.

'No shower, sorry, but you're welcome to go upstairs and use the main bathroom when you feel up to it.'

'This is fine,' she assured him. 'What a fabulous old bath.'

'The feet look a bit rusty.' David poked one of the cast iron claws with his foot, sending flakes of rust onto cracked linoleum. He turned a big, brass tap on and a stream of rusty water came out. Something clanged ominously within the walls.

'Maybe this isn't such a good idea,' he muttered.

'No...' The prospect of David changing his mind was disturbing. Now that Anne had made the difficult decision she wanted to be here. Kind of. 'Look...the water's coming clear now. It just hasn't been used for a while.'

'There's a plumber due tomorrow to have a look at things. There's someone coming from an electrical firm as well. I used the time you were in ED to make a few calls and found a representative from an interior design company who's keen to come and do a quote. She says they've won all sorts of awards for their restoration work. They all know I've left a key for them outside but I hope they won't disturb you too much.'

'No problem.' Anne moved back to her bedroom. The suitcase David had carried in was on the floor beside the old brass bed. 'Do I need some linen?'

'I'll take care of that.'

The thought of David tucking in sheets and putting fresh cases on the pillows for her was embarrassing. Too personal. The tension in the room suddenly escalated.

'You need to rest,' he reminded her. 'Hauling things around or lifting heavy stuff is not on the agenda.'

Anne couldn't help smiling.

'Hey! I'm not joking here.'

'I know. Thank you for your concern.'

His eyes were still narrowed suspiciously. 'So why were you smiling?'

'You sounded as stern as Mac and Julia did back when I first got pregnant. It always amused me because I felt like I'd spent my whole life worrying about Jules. It was a bit of a U-turn to have her fussing over me.'

Special, though, to have someone so concerned about her physical well-being. To feel so cared for.

'I'm not fussing,' David assured her. 'Just being sensible. I don't want to be scooping you up and carting you back to the emergency department again.'

'Perish the thought.' One that was even more embarrassing than having household chores like changing bed linen being done on her behalf.

Was David also embarrassed by the reminder of being forced to hold her in his arms for so long? The silence certainly felt horribly awkward.

'I haven't even thanked you for rescuing me.'

David shrugged. 'Just in the right place at the right time, I guess. Now, why don't you find the kitchen and make sure you'll be able to find everything you need in the morning? It'll only take me a minute to sort this lot out.'

Obediently, Anne made a slow circuit of the ground floor. Things were just as she remembered them in the big, farmhouse-style kitchen. A glance into the refrigerator was a surprise. So was the pantry.

'You look like you've prepared for a siege,' she said when she returned to her room to find David stuffing the last pillow into a fresh white case. 'So much food!'

'Mmm.' David put the pillow down and gave it a prod. 'I've discovered the convenience of online shopping. Guess I went a bit overboard.'

No surprises there for a man who loved to plan things in meticulous detail. He was like that in his work, too. Nothing got missed. He'd wanted to plan his future like that, too, hadn't he? To make sure he didn't miss out on anything. Like a family.

Again, the silence was awkward. So full of shards of the past that had to be avoided to risk injury.

David cleared his throat. 'It's getting late. I'll leave you to settle in. I put towels in the bathroom.'

'Thanks.'Exhaustion was setting in. The aftermath of the physical and mental roller-coaster she'd been on for days now. Anne eyed the high bed and soft looking pillows. 'Sleep is looking like a very good idea.'

David turned back again as he was going through the doorway. He wasn't smiling but there was a softening to his face that deepened the lines around his eyes and made his lips look fuller. Softer. A kind of precursor to a smile. Or a kiss…

'I'm only upstairs,' he said. 'If you need any help in the night.'

Anne opened her eyes to bright sunlight coming in through windows she had neglected to pull curtains on. The moment of wondering where the hell she was turned into astonishment that she must have fallen into a deep and dreamless sleep the instant her head had touched those wonderful feather pillows.

She felt rested. So much better, in fact, it was a shock to find her head reeling when she tried to stand up. It took a good minute for the dizziness to recede but making it to the bathroom and finding that her bleeding had virtually ceased made up for feeling as weak as a kitten. The pain had gone from her belly as well. Even her breasts felt much less tender.

Not that she had time for more than a quick physical self-assessment. A glance at her watch made her jaw drop. She had slept for nearly twelve hours and it was 9:30 a.m. She would be lucky to have time to make herself look respectable and find time for a coffee before the first of the contractors arrived.

There was an eerie silence to the house when she made her way to the kitchen. David would be long gone. Had he felt her presence in the house this morning, the way she was aware of his absence?

Maybe. There was a note held onto the fridge door with a smiley magnet button.

Checked on you before I left, it said. *Didn't want to wake you. Be home around 7 p.m. Call or text if you need to.*

He'd checked on her? Been in her bedroom and watched her sleeping? For how long? The thought of him standing in the same room while she had been in bed created a warmth that moved from her belly right up into her cheeks. It wasn't embarrassment this time. It was…

Not something she was going to analyse. She read the note again instead. It finished with his mobile phone number but she had no intention of interrupting his working day if she could help it.

She almost changed her mind less than an hour later.

'What sort of fittings are going in?' The plumber had come looking for her.

'What do you mean?'

'Well, you can go reproduction. Some of it's lovely stuff, like copper cisterns and slippers baths and the like. But if you're looking to modernise, it will affect the pipes. You can conceal cisterns in the wall, for instance. And have a hanging loo that leaves a gap underneath. Easier for cleaning around, you know? Any idea which way you might be heading?'

Anne had to shake her head. 'Sorry but it's not up to me. I can make a note and get the owner to call you.'

'Oh…' the plumber looked disconcerted. 'I thought you were the missus.'

Whatever could have given him that idea?

Had it been because she'd complied with his request on arrival to show him where the main bathroom was? Had something shown in her body language? It had been impossible not to have those flashbacks to the first time David had ever led her up that magnificent sweep of ornate wooden staircase. Holding her hand. Stopping, too many times to count, to kiss her senseless on their way to his bedroom.

'No,' she told him. 'I'm just a friend.'

It was surprisingly easy to say. After a good

night's sleep, the implications of that word had changed again. Become something if not desirable then acceptable.

Better than nothing, anyway.

Anne found a pad of paper and a pen and noted all the plumber's immediate queries. He went off to measure the pipes and a couple from an interior design firm arrived. They sailed around the house, becoming progressively more enthusiastic and bouncing ideas off each other after the initial, somewhat awed inspection.

They ended up in the main living room. A wonderful, warm room with a fireplace big enough to roast the proverbial ox, ancient but supremely comfortable leather couches and armchairs and French doors that opened to a terrace and the garden beyond.

It was a room Anne had always loved so it was too hard not to stop and eavesdrop as she went past on her way back to her room.

'It's divine,' the slightly effeminate voice of the male decreed. 'The feature ceiling. That fireplace!'

'The stained glass is fabulous,' the woman added. 'But it's all so dark. Positively medieval.'

'It's the wood. And those dark drapes. Ugh!'

'We could paint the window frames. And the fireplace. Cover the floor.'

'Get rid of all this antique furniture. It's so masculine it's virtually *phallic*.'

'White on white,' the woman said dreamily.

'Oh….oh, yes, darling. I'm loving it.'

'The fireplace would be the feature.'

'Yes. *Yes*. I'm seeing it full of… Ooh, silver spheres.'

Anne had to walk away. She definitely needed to lie down for a while. What on earth was David thinking?

Part of that first afternoon was taken up talking to the insurance assessor. The carpets in her cottage would be lifted tomorrow but he couldn't be sure what was happening underneath. Some of the boards felt suspiciously spongy. Tiles in the kitchen were lifting as well. They would have to be taken up.

'It might take a few days to get things dry enough to do anything,' he warned.

The prognosis sounded bleak enough to make being able to escape into the glorious tangle of David's garden, and not think about any of it for a while, a blessing. There was almost an acre of lawns and trees that had one of the city's small rivers as a boundary. Paths through herbaceous borders led to secret corners and there were any number of lovely nooks to sit in. Or there had been. Some of them were so overgrown only a patch of a stone or wooden bench or a sliver of a pathway flagstone could be seen.

Meeting the landscape architect David had employed negated the pleasure the lengthy ramble had provided. The young man was busy sketching on a large sheet of paper and Anne smiled at his enthusiasm.

'Gorgeous spot, isn't it? This should be an exciting challenge for you.'

'You bet it is. I've never had the chance to work with a house that's crying out for the kind of dramatic foil this one could have.'

'Oh?'All it really needed was to have its original bones uncovered, surely?

'A sweep of lawn, I think, all the way down to the river. Buxus hedging and some gorgeous standards. Bay trees, maybe.'

'Spheres?' Anne suggested drily.

'Exactly. And a water feature. Piped music. Dramatic lighting when we've cleared enough of that jungle from under the trees. That gazebo will have to go, of course. Or get moved. It's completely obstructing the vista from the main entertainment area.'

'The main entertainment area? What's that?'

'I presume he meant the big living room and the terrace.'

'And the vista?' David was popping the tab on a can of chilled lager, having found Anne at the kitchen table with a cup of tea and a notepad full of scribbles.

Her tea was cold now because she'd been sitting in here for an hour, trying not to think about how things might be when David got home. What on earth they could find to talk about that would be safe? The kind of thing that friends might talk about.

She needn't have worried. Reporting back on the visitors to the property was quite enough of a topic.

'The straight line from the terrace to the river,' she explained to David. 'At least, it'll be a straight line once the gazebo gets shifted. Or bulldozed along with the outdated herbaceous borders.'

David put his can down on the old kauri table. He loosened his tie and undid the top button of his shirt. Anne averted her gaze hurriedly but couldn't help the way it was drawn back. Just in time to see him pushing his fingers through his hair. She recognised both the action and the gesture. David was feeling trapped. Unsure. It reminded her of a lion pacing a cage but how much of that tension was to do with what she was telling him? Maybe it was due to her presence. The fact that they were together in a confined space.

'My parents must be rolling over in their graves.

The years my mother spent on making that into a prize-winning garden.' He sat down and sighed. 'What did the decorators have to say?'

Anne didn't need to consult her notes. What she'd overheard had been echoing in her head all afternoon. By the time she finished telling David, he was staring at her in utter bemusement.

'Balls?' he finally muttered. 'They want to fill the fireplace with silver *balls*?'

'Spheres,' Anne corrected. A corner of her mouth twitched.

David held her gaze. 'Balls,' he said again.

Anne couldn't help her unladylike snort of mirth. David held out for a moment longer but then tipped his head back and laughed.

A sound Anne hadn't heard in *so* long.

It opened doors she had avoided, assuming they were locked. Avenues to happy times together. The kind of silliness that could only be engaged in when you were so closely connected to another person that it didn't matter. When you loved them so much that trust was a given.

And then David's head straightened and his gaze brushed hers and then held it. Just for an instant. Long enough to know that he felt that old connection as well. For a heartbeat, they stared at each other. And then they both looked away.

'I'm not having any balls,' David said. 'Inside or out. I'll be telling these people exactly what they can do with their quotes.'

'The plumber wasn't so bad. At least he suggested fittings that would fit the era of the house and restore a bit of its former glory.'

David was silent while he took a long mouthful of his drink.

'That's what I had in mind, I guess. I know this place looks tired and the garden's a mess but I don't want to *change* it. I certainly don't want it to end up looking like some professional template of what's trendy in landscaping or interior design.' His tone softened and became almost wistful. 'I wanted it to look like a home again. Like someone loves it.'

Anne's heart skipped a beat. This mattered.

But why? Was David thinking of living here again? And why should that cause a frisson of excitement? She kept her nod neutral, hoping it was one of sympathy. An encouragement to keep talking, perhaps, but David wasn't looking at her. He was staring at his can of beer and shaking his head.

'There's no point going any further if it's going to be like this. I might as well just put the place on the market as is and let someone else do the restoration.'

'You're *selling*?' The word was a gasp. 'But… you love this place. It's—' She had been going to say 'it's your home' but the words had caught. It wasn't any more, was it?

David still wasn't looking at her. 'You can't always keep the things you love, Annie.' The edges of his words were rough enough to negate the fact that he'd softened her name. They grated, like the way David's chair did as he pushed it roughly back to stand up. 'Sometimes you have to let them go in order to move on. That's life.'

He walked to the fridge and opened the door. Anne found herself staring at his back.

Fighting tears. He hadn't been talking about the house, had he? But it hadn't been an angry statement. Sadness was swirling in her head like a mist his words had created.

And the subject was apparently closed. 'You hungry?'

The query was polite. Friendly, even. 'Not very.'

David looked over his shoulder. 'You need to eat. So do I. How 'bout a steak? And...um...' he peered back into the fridge '...eggs.'

'You don't need to cook for me.'

'I'm cooking for myself. Makes no difference to cook a bit more.'

'Maybe I could help, then. Make a salad or something.'

'Sure. But only if you feel up to it.'

If David was making a deliberate attempt to keep the conversation impersonal while they prepared a meal together, Anne had no objection. It was safe territory and as enjoyable as selecting some of the array of fresh vegetables in the crisper bins to slice up for a salad.

'History suggested a straightforward grand mal seizure,' he related during the second case he was telling her about. 'But there was no history of epilepsy and no apparent triggers.'

'On medication?'

'Only some herbal supplements.'

'No recent head injury?'

'Not even an old one. So I'm thinking, poor woman, this could be the first presentation of some nasty brain lesion and I send her off for a CT and request a neurology consult but they're both clear. We're thinking of discharging her but I'm not happy and then she gets up to go to the loo and guess what?'

'Another seizure?'

'Worse.'

Anne forgot about the red onion she'd been slicing finely. Her jaw dropped. 'She arrested?'

'Yep.'

'What happened?'

'We started resus. About to shock her out of

her VT when she reverted herself and woke up.' She could hear the smile in David's voice as he slid the steaks into a hot pan.

'And?' Anne raised her voice above the sizzle.

'And we got a cardiology consult. Looks like she had a small MI. Enough to put her electrical circuits intermittently out of whack. Could be a congenital conduction abnormality as well. She's been admitted for monitoring and further investigation.'

'So the initial seizure was hypoxic? She'd been non-breathing for long enough?'

'Probably. Maybe the activity of the seizure had been enough to convert the rhythm. Or maybe it was going to happen anyway. She was lucky. Gave my junior staff a good lesson in not taking things entirely at face value, as well. Right. These steaks are done. If you still like yours medium rare, that is?'

Anne nodded. 'They smell fantastic. I think I am hungry after all.'

'Good. Let's eat.'

Conversation ceased after they sat down at the table but it wasn't such an uncomfortable silence this time. Talking about the house and then work had tapped into the kind of communication that had been habitual. A comfort zone. Having a meal together was in that same zone.

Anne was too tired to be really hungry and she'd had enough after only a few mouthfuls. She toyed with her food, thinking about what a different quality her weariness today had compared to last night.

It was only then that it struck her how much her mind had been occupied by things other than her present worries like her body and the babies or even past ones such as David represented. Had she been so appalled at what could be allowed to happen on a remake of this wonderful old house and garden that it had been enough to distract her this much or had her subconscious latched onto it as a means of escape? A chance to rest and heal.

Not that it mattered. The net effect had been a very welcome reprieve. What would happen in a day or two when she returned to her own home? It would be a mess but not one that required imagination to fix. Her brain might be too hormone addled to focus on something academic right now but it needed more activity than simply choosing new carpet or watching tiles being relaid.

And that was when the idea occurred to her.

'I've got a guy who's done a lot of work on my cottage,' she told David. 'Jim. Semi-retired, master builder but he can turn his hand to anything. He'd be perfect for the kind of repairs you need done here, like the windowsills and sticky doors. He could do a bathroom makeover or something, too.'

David was still eating heartily but he paused and swallowed his mouthful. 'Not much point starting if I'm not going to go the whole way.'

'Jim has mates. There's an army of these semi-retired tradesmen out there and I reckon they all drink at the same pub or something. If I give Jim something he can't handle, he can always find someone who can. And they're always good. I had Pete in to do painting and wallpapering a while back and I had no complaints.'

'But I'd still have to make choices about something I'm totally ignorant about. I couldn't pick a colour or a wallpaper pattern to save myself.'

'But I could.'

David's new forkful of food hovered in mid-air. 'Why would you want to?'

'Distraction. My mind is mush. I'd enjoy a project that would keep me busy until I'm well enough to go back to work.'

He was frowning now.

'I'm not suggesting I stay here for weeks, don't worry. I can spend the next day or two thinking and planning and maybe getting fabric and paper samples delivered. It's not that far to my place. I could come over while you're at work and supervise what was being done.'

David was listening now. 'What about the garden?'

'One of my neighbour's sons comes in to do any heavy stuff I need. He's a student and will be on summer break by now. If he hasn't got a job, I'm sure he'd jump at the opportunity.'

'I wouldn't know where to start in telling him what to do.' David was staring at Anne now. 'Would you?'

'Maybe. I'd like to give it a go.'

'But…why?' There was something dark in his gaze now. Wariness, if not mistrust.

Anne took a deep breath. She needed to choose her words carefully and she wasn't entirely sure what it was she wanted to say exactly. It had something to do with the analogy that she'd picked up on when he'd said he was planning to sell the house. That you had to let things go to move on.

'You want someone to love this house, don't you? To make it a real home again.'

His nod was terse.

'Right now it's not at its best. You might get

someone who can't see what it has to offer. Can't see past the…damage, I guess. If you could fix it up and maybe make it even better than it ever was before, you'll find someone who will love it for what it *is*, not what it could be.'

She held her breath. There was no need to hammer the analogy. If there was anything left of that old connection, David would know exactly what she was talking about. What she was offering. A chance at friendship. To repair the damage their relationship might have left them with. Closure perhaps.

Peace.

'Damage does haunt, doesn't it?' he said at last. She could see the movement in his neck as he swallowed. 'We could give it a try, I guess. See how it goes.'

Anne could only nod. She didn't trust herself to speak for a moment. Even if David was prepared to try repairing something more than what their conversation had ostensibly been about, she couldn't afford that tiny spark of hope reigniting. The one that had flared when he'd said *come home with me.*

'I'll call in the troops,' was all she said finally. 'First thing tomorrow.'

CHAPTER SIX

LEARNING that the removal of damaged floor-boards from her cottage had revealed piles in dire need of replacement should have been a cause for dismay.

'I can't move home yet,' she told David. 'Half my floor's been ripped up.'

'Are you in a hurry to get home?'

No. Not if he wanted her to stay...

'Not really. But I didn't intend imposing on you for so long. I could move to a motel or some-thing.'

'You're hardly imposing.' But David shoved his fingers through his hair, unconsciously reveal-ing that the idea of her staying longer might be disturbing. Then he gave her a searching look. Anne said nothing, allowing him time to see whatever it was he was looking for. It only took an instant.

'Seems to me like you've become a project manager in the last few days,' he said. 'For a job I couldn't have tackled to save myself. I should be paying you a lot more than room and board.'

'Don't be daft. I'm having fun.'

Smiling, she waved a hand at the chaos in front of her. The big mahogany table in the dining room was covered with plans for things like an en suite going into the master bedroom and a makeover for the other bathrooms. Sketches of ideas for the garden and paint colour cards were scattered amongst pictures cut from house and garden type magazines. Fabric samples draped the back of chairs and rolls of wallpaper were open and anchored with books on the floor.

This project had become more than fun. At some stage in the last few days Anne had become hooked. She'd never attempted renovation on anything like this scale but then she'd never had the time or the need for distraction. Or an apparently unlimited budget.

Her enthusiasm seemed to be contagious. David returned her smile. 'And I'm enjoying having some company and something happening in the house,' he said. 'It felt like a mausoleum when I first came back. Now it's…'

'A mess?'

'Alive.'

Nothing more had been said about her moving out since then. Day after day went by with the momentum of the renovation project increasing at a pace that mirrored Anne's returning physical well being. She was regaining her emotional strength as well. So much so, that when the prospect of spending a whole day with David when he had his first day off in more than a week was disturbing, Anne decided it was time to stretch her wings.

'I'm going to go and visit Jules and Mac and the babies today,' she informed David when he appeared in the dining room to get an update on progress, a mug of coffee in his hand. 'Daily phone calls don't seem to be enough any more. I'd like to see them all.'

'They live over the back of Governer's Bay, don't they?'

'Yes. Up on the hill with a fabulous view of the harbour.'

'That's quite a drive. You sure you're up to it?'

Anne's nod was confident. 'My car needs a run. The battery's probably getting flat by now.'

'I could drive you over.' Something in his gaze suggested that he hadn't been considering the condition of her vehicle.

'No need,' Anne said hurriedly. Even if he wasn't showing a disconcerting comprehension of how difficult it might be for her to see the babies again, being in car with David would be very different to being in his house like this. Here, there were constant reminders that they weren't alone.

Right now, hammering sounds came from upstairs where Jim and his team were working in the main bathroom. A conversation between a couple of electricians was taking place in the hallway outside what had become Anne's office and through the latticed windows Nick, the university student, gave a wave as he walked past, carrying a serious looking hedge clipper under one arm.

Anne waved back and nodded her approval. The banging overhead got louder.

'It would be a nice drive,' David added. 'I could go for a walk while you were visiting.' He looked up at the ceiling. 'Don't think I'll get much done around here today.'

Anne paused in the sorting of the quotes she'd been reviewing. David might be enjoying how lively the house had become but it had to be unsettling when you couldn't be sure if the water was running or whether a stranger might be in the bathroom you were hoping to use. And maybe it was more to do with him enjoying having company.

Was David lonely?

Like she was a lot of the time when she wasn't at work?

She was going to see her family today. David didn't have any family and he'd always been a bit like her in that his devotion to his career hadn't allowed for the nurturing of close friendships.

When they'd had each other, it hadn't mattered.

'Maybe I'll go and see if I can give that young lad in the garden a hand with something.' David turned to leave and Anne felt the distance stretching between them.

'You're welcome to come with me if you'd like to,' she found herself saying. 'I won't be staying long and I...wouldn't mind a walk somewhere myself.' She rolled her gaze upwards as a particularly loud cracking noise came from directly overhead. 'It is a bit hard to think in here today.'

If Julia and Mac were surprised to see Anne's companion, they hid it well.

'Gidday, mate.' The colloquialism delivered with a strong Scottish accent made them all smile and broke any possibility of ice. 'Come on in.'

Sunshine streamed into the little house on the

hill. The living area was taken over by baby gear. Prams and change tables and nappies. A clothes horse was draped with tiny articles drying in the sunshine. The kitchen bench was cluttered with bottles and measuring spoons and tins of formula.

'Good grief!' Anne exclaimed. 'I'd forgotten how completely babies take over your life.'

'We're living and breathing babies,' Julia said happily. 'It's heaven.'

They were so obviously rapt. Anne had given them this gift and she'd never felt so welcome. She hadn't expected that being bathed in this environment would be so overwhelming, however. The whole house actually *smelled* of baby. Of formula and nappies and damp clothes. It took her back. Way, way back to when the centre of her own life had been her small and helpless baby sister. To when there'd been no time for anything for herself but it hadn't occurred to her to feel put upon in any way because that tiny being had been so important. So precious.

She completely understood the intensity of this

time in Julia and Mac's life. She didn't expect the conversation to include anything other than the twins and it didn't. They talked of feeding patterns and details of mixing formula and sterilising bottles. Of sleeping—or lack of it on the part of the parents—and of how bathtime got organised each evening. Anne was also quite prepared to admire the infants with the kind of reverence their parents demonstrated.

What was even more unexpected, given the overwhelming environment, was the way she was able to take a step back. The way her body and mind were accepting—possibly with a tinge of relief—that these weren't *her* babies. Her heart was squeezed by the force of love she could feel but her breasts gave no more than a tingle of protest that was easily dismissed, and that heaviness in her belly was gone. So different from how she'd felt in the first days after the birth. That counsellor had been right. It had been hard but it had been the right thing to do to create that initial distance.

The bonding of this new family was so

powerful. She wasn't excluded by any means but neither was she in that inner, almost obsessed, circle. She could feel David watching her as she held wee Angus but her smile was genuine.

'He's gorgeous,' she pronounced, handing him back to his dad as he began to grizzle loudly. 'He looks just like you, Mac.'

'He does, doesn't he?' Mac was bursting with pride. 'Chip off the old block.'

'And don't you think Amy looks a bit like me?' Julia asked hopefully. She rocked the baby she was holding as Amy joined her brother in a hungry wail.

'Absolutely.' Anne was still smiling as she noted a hint of a puzzled frown on David's face. He was shifting his gaze from each baby to its parent, clearly making an attempt to find the likeness. Her smile faded as the babies increased the intensity of their demanding cries. She could feel the sound closing in around her. She needed to *do* something. Now.

'There, there, darling,' Julia soothed. 'Lunch is on its way. Mac?'

'Onto it. Come on soldier.' He shifted Angus so that the baby was upright on his shoulder. 'Let's mix that formula.'

'Do...you need a hand?'

'No. We've got this down to a fine art. Unless you want to hang around and help feed them?'

Something like panic edged into the tension. Anne opened her mouth to speak but David answered first.

'I promised Anne lunch somewhere nice. And a walk. If we don't go now we might miss the best of the day weather-wise.'

Julia nodded but her eyes held a question.

Anne hugged her gently, enclosing the baby in the space between them. 'Next time,' she whispered.

'You okay?' The words were almost inaudible.

'I'm good.' Anne tightened the hug a fraction. 'But baby steps, yes?'

She turned to let David know she was ready to leave but he was already heading for the door. Implementing her rescue. Had he been aware that she was reaching her emotional limits? Did he understand, even a little? It was a powerful notion. One that was giving her an ally. A friend. It felt like another bit of tarnish was being polished off the connection between them, making it shine like gold.

The need to escape had been puzzling but real.

Talk about full on!

Still feeling somewhat in shock, David said little as they got back into the car and drove further around the harbour. Some fine tuning of his preconceptions clearly needed to be done.

The experience of the last hour or so wasn't at all what he remembered of encounters with children, which was odd, given that he'd had plenty of contact over the years. Paediatric patients and their siblings, children of colleagues that appeared, albeit briefly, at dinner parties. Had he chosen to only remember some of them in order to fashion his own desires for the future? Or maybe he'd only registered the ones who were old enough to communicate. The ones who had their own personalities. Small people.

Of course, he knew they'd all been newborns at some stage. He'd assumed he had a handle on that as well but given the taste of reality he'd just experienced, his notions were kind of fuzzy around the edges. Had he been spared most of the details by doting parents and nurses who had attended to physical necessities?

'Do all new parents do that?' he asked Anne as they stopped at a corner shop, having decided that the day was nice enough for a picnic.

'What?'

'Talk about what they find in nappies, for instance, as if it was genuinely fascinating?'

'Yeah.' Anne slanted him an amused glance. 'What goes in and comes out of those little creatures is absolutely riveting. So is every twitch and burp and analysis of any differences in the noises they make. It's all part of the bonding process.'

'More like an obsession.' David led the way into the shop. 'I guess it's nature's way of ensuring survival.'

'It's like falling in love,' Anne said quietly, from behind him. 'When you're the one involved, it's as natural as breathing.'

The bonding theory to ensure survival made sense. But if it was instinctive, why hadn't Anne experienced it after giving birth? Or maybe she had. She'd said as much, hadn't she? He'd been so prepared to slate her for giving those babies away and then turning her back on them and she'd stunned him when she'd said she couldn't go and stay with her sister because she wanted to see the babies *too* much.

And…maybe hope had been born in that instant. Hope that there could be a future for them that gave both of them what they wanted most in life. He wasn't ready to go down that track, however. Not when it might mean setting himself up for the kind of heartbreak he'd spent a year getting over. Not when Anne wasn't herself. They were both vulnerable. Confused. What fate had provided, in their living arrangements, was a kind of breathing space.

Determined to let the topic drop, David parked

again at a small bay where a strip of grass led down to a rocky beach. There was a wooden table with built-in benches that was ideal for sitting at to eat the sandwiches and fruit they had purchased. The air smelled of the kelp that was piled up on the rocks below and the sun was warm enough to invite a scramble amongst the rock pools when they had finished eating.

It was Anne who voiced thoughts that were still focused on that visit.

'Poor Mac,' she murmured, watching a family of crabs scuttle into hiding having been disturbed by a shifting rock. 'I don't think he's too keen on having to go back to work next week when his paternity leave runs out.'

David made a sound of agreement but somewhere in the back of his mind another mental rock had been dislodged. Paternity leave? Had it ever occurred to him that he might want to take advantage of such a thing when he had a newborn of his own? Weeks of time away from work? How disruptive would that be? He'd assumed that the mother would be more than willing to make that kind of a sacrifice, though, hadn't he?

Finding a large, smooth, sun-warmed boulder, David sat down to watch Anne crouching to peer into the rock pool.

'He does seem just as enthralled as Julia.'

'He's a natural-born dad.' Picking up a stick of driftwood, Anne poked gently at a sea anemone to watch it flutter shut. 'I know how he feels,' she said a moment later. 'I used to hate having to go to school and leave Jules with the nanny.'

The loose braid of Anne's dark hair lay across her back as she leaned forward, the sun bringing out tiny sparkles of light that made it come alive. Tendrils had come loose and the breeze made them play against her neck and face. David had to fight the urge to reach out and smooth them back. He wanted to see—and touch—the milky smoothness of that skin. It was good to see her relaxing like this, with a childlike fascination for what the rock pool contained.

Such a contrast to the focused energy he'd always associated with her. The sort that was intrinsic to her work and was showing again now in the absorption with the project of restoring his house. The capable, impressive side of Anne Bennett. He'd known her history of raising her sister but had he ever really considered the effect it might have had? Had she really been in the same space that Julia and Mac currently inhabited?

'But you were just a kid,' he said aloud. 'What, six or seven years old?'

'I became a mother.' Anne sat down on the rocks. Her knees were bent and her arms went around them as though she was curling up to comfort herself. And she still stared into the rock pool.

'I was holding her when Mum died,' she said softly. 'Did I ever tell you that?'

'No, I don't think so.'

Anne sighed. 'It was terrifying. But kind of wonderful in a weird way. Taking responsibility for that little baby and looking after her was what got me through the grief. And Dad understood that. He helped but it was always him helping me, not the other way round.'

'And you were still a teenager when you lost your dad, weren't you? That must have been very hard.'

Anne gave a slow nod. 'I was seventeen. Just finishing school and ready to go to uni. Old enough to be able to keep us together without Social Services stepping in and putting Jules in a foster-home, thank goodness.'

The disruption of paternity leave was nothing compared to what Anne had done for her family. It touched him now, as it always had. Maybe it had been her stunning looks and what he'd seen of her skills as a doctor that had attracted him in the first place but knowing her unusual history had certainly contributed to him falling in love with this woman.

She was so capable. So independent. And, at the same time so incredibly giving.

She was still that same person. Even if she couldn't give him what *he* wanted.

Maybe he had been wrong. It was quite possible

that he and Anne could be together again. All he had to do was tell her that he'd changed his mind. That being with her was all that mattered. In the wake of that visit to the twins, he could probably sound convincing in admitting he hadn't really thought it through. That maybe he wasn't ready for that kind of disruption to his life. Maybe he would never be ready.

They could both continue their high-powered careers unchecked. They would understand the pressure the other was under and be able to support and nurture success. They would be wealthy enough to have the best of everything. A dream home. Luxurious holidays anywhere they chose. Freedom to choose any hobby they fancied—if they ever found the time.

And perhaps that was the crux. Maybe they wouldn't need or want to find the time for anything as frivolous as a hobby. Life would be two-dimensional. Each other…and work. Quite apart from watching the joy of children growing up, having a family made finding time a priority. It would give life new dimensions. New meaning. Make it bigger, somehow and more worthwhile.

Was it being selfish, wanting it all? Everything that life had to offer that was good and meaningful?

He had the possibility of a choice here. To be with the woman he loved or to have the family he dreamed of. He was the one who would have to make the sacrifice, though, and he wasn't ready to do that. Despite this overwhelming awareness of the person he knew Anne to be. She wasn't the only one who'd worked hard to get where she was. Who knew what she wanted the future to hold? Whether or not she would be part of that future, however, she deserved to know how special she was.

'You are amazing, you know,' he said quietly. 'What you've done for Julia has been truly extraordinary.'

'You mean the surrogacy thing?'

'That, too.' He had to touch her. To try and release what was tying him into a knot inside.

He held out his hand. 'You had enough fresh air? Don't want you to overdo things.'

Anne took his hand and let him help her to her feet. The rocky surface was uneven, though, and she stumbled. Fell into his arms.

The opportunity was irresistible. David held her and let her get her balance. He waited until she looked up at him, with a mixture of relief and...surprise in her face. Her eyes shone and her lips were parted a little. And her hands were clinging to his shoulders. David didn't wait for common sense to override his response. He bent his head and kissed her.

It was a gentle kiss.

A brief, soft touch of David's lips to her own. Anne didn't have time to close her eyes, even, so she was still looking up at him, stunned, when he pulled back.

For a heartbeat, they simply looked at each other, saying nothing.

Anne could feel her heart hammering but it had nothing to do with the fright of her near fall seconds ago. She could still feel David's hands cradling her back as well, steadying her. And she could feel the strength in the muscles beneath her hands because she was still clutching his upper arms.

She could hear the roll of gentle waves on rocks below and the jagged edge to the breath David was drawing in.

She could smell something more potent than the salt water in the surrounding rock pools or the piles of kelp further away. The same smell she remembered from being carried in David's arms when she'd been barely conscious. The alluring scent of safety.

Her lips were still tingling from that brief touch of his. A sensation that was opening new memories. Awakening desire. She could *taste* it.

Oh…*help*!

She should move, Anne decided in that split second of being aware of little other than what her senses were telling her. She could actually feel the message being sent to her body. An order for action. It complied, sort of. It just seemed to move in the wrong direction.

Closer to David.

An infinitesimal amount, maybe, but it was enough for David to notice. For him to respond by drawing her even closer. Enough to prompt him to bend his head again, and this time it was a real kiss.

His lips moved over hers with the subtle changes of position and pressure that were a familiar form of communication. It was impossible not to slip straight back into a response that begged for more. For what she knew he was capable of giving her.

Such intense pleasure. Sensations that made her forget she had bones in her body. That made things sparkle and curl deep inside. Tiny lights she hadn't felt for a very long time. A brightness she knew could be turned up until it exploded.

God, she had missed this.

The kiss went on. And on. For too long. For not nearly long enough.

Anne wasn't sure who pulled away first. The

one whose common sense had called loudly enough to be heard, perhaps. Those lights began to dim and flicker, leaving her feeling curiously bereft. And shocked at how bright they had been. Was it her own reaction she could see in David's eyes when she met them this time? Or was he feeling the same way?

Who would have thought that the time apart from each other could have magnified physical attraction to that degree? That they were not only still fluent in that very private language but that it seemed to be on an entirely new level.

A dangerous level.

One that made Anne think crazy thoughts.

Like the fact that having those babies for Julia had shown her she was quite capable of being a mother again. That the tape had been peeled away from a maternal switch she had been sure would not be turned on again. That giving birth and nurturing her own child could be fulfilling in a way her career might never be.

That she could have David's baby.

And David.

But part of her mind was fighting back. Pushing opposing thoughts into her head. The kind she had been convinced were the truth when she had given those babies to their real mother. That she had already sacrificed enough. That this was *her* time. The only time she might have in her entire life when she could reach out and achieve her own dreams.

Amazing how fast thoughts could flash. How what was happening in your head could be so at war with what was happening in your heart. And body. No wonder it created a kind of meltdown. A feeling of utter confusion.

Could David see all that happening in the tiny space of time he continued to hold her, with both his hands and his gaze? Was that why she could see what looked like a reflection of her own confusion?

Anne could only be grateful that David took charge of what could have become an awkward moment.

His lips curved in a smile. 'Oops,' he said. 'Where did that come from?'

She could have said something that might have revealed the effect that kiss had had on her. She was tempted to say that she didn't care where it had come from as long as they could find their way back again.

But that would lead to talking about it. She might confess her confusion and even suggest that she'd been wrong about what she wanted in her future.

And what if David didn't want what he had once wanted? He was selling his beloved property. He had a new job lined up to go to very soon. He'd moved on.

This last year hadn't been a picnic for either of them. Was it fair to start something that might simply be a re-run of the past? A relationship that promised everything but disintegrated into the pain of two people pulling in different directions and ripping little pieces off the other as they did so.

Anne couldn't face that. Especially not now when she knew very well that she was more emotionally fragile than she had ever been in her life before. The prospect of adding that kind of pain was terrifying.

So she simply smiled back at David as she began easing herself away from his touch.

'Sea air,' she said lightly. 'It's known for its freshness.'

She took a shaky breath and discovered she could move properly now. She turned to start the short trek back to her car. 'I think you were right,' she added. 'I shouldn't overdo things.'

'Had enough, then?' David's voice was right behind her. His words very quiet.

She chose to ignore the ambiguity in his query.

Or maybe she didn't.

'Yes,' was all she said.

'Fine.'

She couldn't see David's face so she had to guess at what the tone of that word revealed. The best she could come up with was, what... resignation?

'Let's go home,' he added.

No. Not resignation. It was more like relief.

CHAPTER SEVEN

A WEEK went by and some shape began to emerge from the chaos of restoration work on David's house and garden.

Basic repairs had been completed. New plumbing and wiring was in place. Old paintwork was spruced up and faded wallpaper stripped from many rooms. In the garden, new leaves and buds were already appearing to fill in the raw patches where shrubs and roses had been pruned, and the borders had fresh, newly turned soil in places that had only been a tangle of weeds recently.

The weather was glorious and every day Anne could open windows all over the house to let sunshine and fresh air reach every corner and counteract the dust and dirt from the ongoing work. She was making final choices for new wallpaper and curtain fabrics. She had discovered garden centres and filled trolleys with boxes of bedding plants or chosen rose bushes from the glossy pictures on the nursery walls.

The promise of what the finished picture would be like hung in the air, taking shape and urging her to become a little more involved with every passing day. David seemed to be enjoying the process as much as Anne was. He opened accounts at plant nurseries and fabric stores.

'Are you sure you don't want to put a limit on what you're spending?' Anne had to check one day during the following week, having had a wonderful afternoon choosing baby trees.

He shook his head. 'Go for it,' he told her. 'You're doing an amazing job. I think you missed your vocation.'

'I am loving it,' she admitted. 'I never even knew I was interested in this kind of thing.'

'You should be resting, not scraping paint and lugging stuff around. For heaven's sake, Annie, you were holding a *spade* when I got home today and you'd obviously been using it.'

'I needed some exercise. I'm feeling fine. Never

better, in fact.' And it was true but her smile had more to do with the way David had said her name than her physical well-being. They were in this project together and it was drawing them a little closer every day. 'You know what they say,' she added.

'What?'

'A change is as good as a holiday.'

'Some holiday.'

'Works for me. This is the longest I've ever had away from work and I'm not remotely bored.'

'Really?' David's glance was curious. 'Aren't you missing work at all?'

'Not yet.' Surprisingly, this was also true. There was something vaguely disturbing about that but Anne wasn't going to try and analyse what that might be. 'I'm sure I will once this project is finished.'

'Mmm.' David suddenly seemed absorbed in sorting the handful of mail he'd brought inside with him. 'I'm sure you will.'

The moment had been loaded with…something. Again, Anne didn't want to try and figure out what it was because there was something else hanging in the air these days.

That kiss on the beach.

It hadn't been mentioned. It certainly hadn't been repeated but it was there. A different kind of promise, maybe.

But of what?

Anne was trying to ignore it. Trying not to ignite any spark of hope that it was a doorway back to a relationship that might be more than friendship. The kind of spark she'd experienced when David had suggested she come home with him. She wasn't even sure she wanted a repeat of that kiss, despite the messages her body gave her when she lay alone in her bed at night but even if she did, the first move would have to come from David.

He was the one who'd pulled a plug on the relationship in the first place. He hadn't been prepared to compromise on his dreams for his future and he'd made decisive moves to get on with his life. He still was making those moves with his plans to sell his property. If the kiss had changed anything, Anne was sure she would pick up on it and that would be the time to start seriously thinking about where they were headed.

And maybe that was why that particular moment had seemed so loaded. She'd been unable to stop herself looking for clues. David had seemed astonished she wasn't missing work and that she was enjoying the domestic kind of challenge she had taken on with the house and garden. Was he thinking she might be happy to give up work for a longer time and be content to nurture children as well as a garden? Had she been encouraging that line of thought with her accounts of happy visits to see Julia and Mac and the twins over the last couple of weeks? There was no mistaking the way David had lost interest in the conversation when she'd said she would start missing work in due course.

Let it go, she ordered herself. This kind of mental circuit was useless. Damaging. Something had changed for the better in the wake of that kiss because they were more comfortable with each other and Anne was more than happy not to rock the boat. Despite the rapidly increasing level of her physical activity, she *was* still resting emotionally. Content to sidestep both the kind of fierce mental effort her job involved and also the emotional roller-coaster that came with the territory of an intimate relationship.

It was a joy to have a distraction that was both compelling and deeply satisfying. And maybe the promise hanging in the air was the same for both aspects of her life right now—the restoration project and her relationship with David. Basic repairs had been done. The finished picture was unknown but was drawing them both forward because it had to be better than it had been before.

Toward the end of that week, Anne was spending the last of the daylight to empty some of the numerous boxes of plants she had purchased. This was the best time of day for this task. Hot sun would not stress the baby plants. She could give them a good drink and they would have the whole night to settle into their new environment.

This was one of the bigger borders, in view of the main living area.

'Part of the vista,' she reminded herself with a giggle.

Her plan had been simple. She wanted to create a colourful mass of blooms. The kind that David's mother had probably taken pride in. After consulting books and experts in the garden centres, she was planting old-fashioned flowers en masse.

Plants like delphiniums and hollyhocks for height at the back, nigella and aquilegia amongst the rose bushes in the middle and a border of gorgeous blue violas along the front.

The house was empty.

So quiet.

Disappointment at not finding Anne in the kitchen where she normally was at this time of day morphed into something even less pleasant as a horrible notion occurred to David.

Maybe she'd packed her bags and gone home. She might have had a phone call today to tell her that the repairs on her cottage were complete and it was ready for habitation again. She might have tried to call him to tell him she was moving home but he'd been so busy he hadn't even glanced at his cellphone for too many hours to count and then the idea of checking for messages had been the last thing on his mind when all he'd wanted had been to get home and unwind after a frantic day.

It had been one major case after another in the emergency department today. A child had been knocked from his bicycle by a careless motorist and the head injury had looked serious enough to have panic-stricken parents and other relatives haunting the department until the little boy had been stabilised and taken to the intensive care unit. A man of only thirty-five had been the victim of a major heart attack and had arrested twice before he could be stabilised enough to be transferred into the care of cardiologists and taken to the catheter laboratory where several stents had been put in to repair blocked arteries.

Another adult had presented with terrifying shortness of breath that turned out to be a pulmonary embolus complicating the recovery from recent surgery. And amidst all the major drama had been the relentless stream of less life-threatening but still serious cases. People who had been in pain and sick and needed medical assistance.

Yes, it had been an exceptionally long day but David had been completely in his element. It might have been stressful and tiring but even in its most chaotic moments he'd been aware of an undercurrent that had added to his job satisfaction. One that he hadn't really been aware of missing for rather a long time.

That undercurrent was the knowledge that at the end of his day he would be going home to someone who would be genuinely interested in hearing all about it.

Funny how that extra dimension could make such a difference. Enough to make it no chore to spend even longer at work. Long enough to make a visit to the intensive care unit and the coronary care unit to follow up on some of those patients so that he could add to their stories when telling them to Anne.

But she wasn't here.

David dropped his briefcase beside the kitchen table, shrugged off his jacket to throw it over the back of a chair and loosened the tie that was starting to feel like a noose around his neck. He wrenched open the door of the fridge and extracted a bottle of icy-cold lager, flipping off the lid and not bothering to pick it up when it skated across the bench to land in the sink.

Moodily, he wandered out of the kitchen. The door to the guest suite was open but he could sense the emptiness beyond. When he'd finished his beer, he'd better unearth his phone and find out where the hell Anne had gone. With a sigh that was more like a low-grade rumble, he skirted the heap of drop sheets and big buckets that were obviously awaiting the return of the decorators in the morning. Their presence prompted him to walk into the main living area in the hope that some visible progress might spark an interest that seemed to have utterly faded since noticing he was alone in the house.

Wallpapering had begun. The huge room looked ghostly in the fading daylight thanks to the pale drop sheets covering all the furniture and the lack of any curtains at the windows. Ghostly and…lonely. He could brighten things up by turning on some lights but why bother? Taking another long swig of his drink, David stepped towards the remaining natural light instead. More out of a sense of duty than interest he looked through the latticed windows to see if he could spot anything new in the garden re-development.

And there, right in front of him, he saw Anne crouched on the edge of the biggest border.

Thank God, was his first thought. *She's still here.*

The wash of relief was powerful enough to render him motionless, his drink poised in mid-air. He felt his lips curl into a smile that was entirely unconscious and then both his hand and his eyelids lowered as something much darker than relief took over.

Dismay.

Why did it have to be *this* woman who provoked such overwhelmingly strong feelings in him?

Would he ever be able to get over her?

Did he want to?

Opening his eyes again, David found it was still bright enough outside to make him blink. It would be light for maybe another hour but the sun was low enough to be casting a rosy tinge of sunset on everything, making it look warmer. Softer. Very, very inviting. And Anne was central to that scene.

She was totally intent on her task. She wouldn't have been able to see him standing here, staring at her, anyway, with the sun reflecting off the windows so there was no reason for her to have been distracted. Or for David to move. He could indulge himself for a minute or two and watch her easing tiny plants from a container, cradling each one in her hands before setting it into a hole she had already made in the freshly turned soil. He could see the care she took in positioning them and then pressing earth gently around each new plant.

She'd obviously been out there for some time. The whole border was dotted with small, fragile-looking green clumps. Her arms and face were streaked with dirt and he saw why when she pushed wayward tendrils of hair back from her face before reaching for another plant.

Maybe she was so absorbed with what she was doing that she had simply lost track of the time. She needed to stop. To eat and rest. Unaware of his decisive nod, David headed for the door.

The ache in her back intensified as Anne finally stood up to drop the last, empty punnet into the wheelbarrow. She arched backwards, her hands on her hips to dig her fingers into the spot that hurt, and then she straightened, letting her breath out slowly.

A contented sigh.

She was tired, yes, and her back was a bit

sore, but apart from that she was feeling great. Fantastic, even. The satisfaction she was getting out of the creative enterprise of the last few weeks was something new and extraordinary. She couldn't wait to show David what she'd accomplished today and share the vision of what it was going to look like in a season or two.

Not that either of them would see the finished picture.

Anne pushed the negative thought aside. How stupid would it be to spoil how good she was feeling right now? Walking towards the nearby tap that had the hose coiled over it was enough to flip the direction of her mood. She dragged in a lungful of the fresh air and noted the spring in her step. She was, possibly, more physically fit than she'd ever been thanks to all the fresh air and exercise in the garden. Hard to believe it was only coming up to a month since she'd given birth to the twins. She'd never expected to recover this quickly, although her back was reminding her that her abdominal muscles still needed a bit more time.

Excess weight was dropping off fast too and that thought made Anne realise how hungry she was. As soon as she'd watered in the new plants she would go inside and start dinner. Having left her watch off, she could only guess at the time but daylight was definitely fading now.

Why wasn't David home yet?

The niggle of concern increased as Anne uncoiled the hose and turned the tap on. It made her turn her head as she pulled the hose towards the garden and it was then she saw him emerge from the house. He had unbuttoned the cuffs of his shirt and was rolling up his sleeves. His tie was gone and the collar was also unbuttoned. His long legs covered the lawn in easy strides and as he got closer Anne could see he was smiling. It was a picture of a man happy to be where he was and doing what he doing.

Something warm curled inside Anne and made her forget any weariness or sore muscles as she smiled back. Had she really thought she was feeling great after that stretch?

She'd been wrong.

This was what feeling great was.

Watching David walk towards her. Feeling like everything was right in the world again. Feeling like she'd arrived home.

Which was stupid. It was David who was arriving home. She didn't really belong here and she wouldn't be here for very much longer. Her smile fading, Anne twisted the nozzle of the hose to send a stronger spray to reach the back of the border.

'Hi,' she called over her shoulder. 'How was work?'

'Flat out.' David stopped beside her and a quick glance showed Anne the glow of sunset on his bare arms as he finished rolling up a sleeve. His hands seemed to glow as well. She'd always loved David's hands. Those long fingers. The mix of strength and cleverness. The ability they had to touch so gently...

She dragged her gaze away. 'Anything interesting?'

'Heaps. I'll tell you all about it over dinner.

Speaking of which, have you got any idea of the time?'

'Not really.' Right now, Anne couldn't think of anything other than David's presence beside her. The huge garden around them seemed to have shrunk. Or vanished. It was like a bubble had formed that enclosed herself and this man and there wasn't quite enough air inside it to make breathing easy. Not when that kiss that had been hanging between them had got trapped in the bubble as well. She took a sideways step and pretended to concentrate on where she was directing the water. 'Nick went home a while ago,' she added. 'And he did say something about it being "food o'clock".'

'How long have you been out here?'

'Since lunch.'

'Good grief! You must be exhausted.'

She could feel him looking at her. Taking in her dirty shorts and mud-caked knees. Her hair hadn't seen a brush in way too long either and Anne was suddenly too aware of how scruffy she must look. She didn't *do* scruffy. Never had. It made her feel out of control somehow. Vulnerable.

'We've got heaps done.' She reached for a verbal anchor. Security. 'I got this border sorted and Nick attacked the hedges again. He found a gap that had grown over.' Anne turned sideways, still gripping the hose. 'It leads to a bit that I didn't even know was there. It's round.'

'What is? The gap?'

'No. The bit behind it. It used to be a lawn. Nick cut the grass and got rid of some old compost bins and started on the inside of the hedges and it was then we could see how round it was.'

David had walked around her to the end of the border and then he stopped and stood very still. 'I'd forgotten it was even here.'

'It was overgrown to the point of vanishing. Or was it a secret garden?'

'No...' David seemed lost in thought. 'It was...a pond.'

'Really?' Forgetting about that dangerous bubble, Anne went to stand beside him, the stream of the hose leaving the garden and pointing to the grass beside her feet.

'It got filled in. It was after Dad died and I think something went wrong with the plumbing and the water drained off and the fish died and Mum didn't have the heart to sort it out. Said she didn't want a pond any more.'

'Oh…' Anne could imagine a water feature tucked away in the quiet, hedge-lined circle. The image was enticing. So enticing she forgot she was even holding the hose until David let out a yelp.

'Oi! My feet don't need watering.'

'Oh, sorry.' Anne tried to turn the hose off but twisted the nozzle in the wrong direction. The jet became a thin line and, to her dismay, it created a hole in the turf, which began to lift. 'Oh, help! I'm ruining the lawn now.'

'Here.' David took the hose from her hands but instead of turning it off he kept it pointing to the same spot. 'Look at that.'

Anne looked. The turf was lifting in a larger piece now.

'It's a paving stone, see?'

'Kind of, I guess.'

David was staring through the gap in the hedge again. He looked back at his feet and then over his shoulder, at the wheelbarrow full of empty plant containers and garden tools.

Moving swiftly, he turned off and abandoned the hose, picking up a spade. With a few decisive sweeps he scraped the turf clear to reveal a large, natural stone paving slab.

'There was a path,' he told Anne, his words tumbling out swiftly. 'And the pond was built of the same kind of stone. There were waterlilies and goldfish and...and it was...just lovely.'

He was looking at her and something in his face made her heart squeeze so hard it was painful. Something poignant. Like loss. She wanted to wrap her arms around him and offer comfort.

Instead, she found herself offering words. 'We could bring it back,' she said softly. 'Make it lovely again.'

There was something else in David's face now. Something that looked like surprise that the possibility might exist. And then hope. And then gratitude for her having thought of it.

It looked a lot like…love.

Maybe it was a trick of the fading light. Anne turned away hurriedly before she could think she saw something that might make her say or do something they might both regret.

David was still staring at her. The tension was unbearable. The bubble was back. So was that kiss. She was getting sucked in. Trapped. If she didn't step out now, she wouldn't be able to.

'I'll…um…get Nick to have a poke around tomorrow, shall I?'

The tension went up a notch but David said nothing. Instead, he seemed to channel the tension into action. He dug his spade into the soil again and Anne heard the clunk of metal striking stone. He walked on a step and repeated the action. Again and again, until the spade made no sound. By now they were well inside the hedge circle and Anne hadn't even noticed she had been following.

'This is it,' David announced. 'The edge of the

pond. I'm pretty sure it was lined with stone as well.' He dug out a spadeful of earth and threw it to one side.

'You're not really dressed for digging,' Anne pointed out.

'I don't care. I want to see if I'm right. This is…' David was grinning. Looking so happy Anne had to grin back at him.

'Archeology?' she suggested. She was catching something here. The joy of discovery perhaps. The excitement of finding something that had been lost.

'It's amazing.' David nodded. 'Like I'm unearthing a bit of my childhood I'd completely forgotten.'

'It's going to get dark soon.'

'This won't take long.'

'There's another spade. I'll help.'

'You shouldn't be doing heavy stuff like this.'

'I'm fine, David. Never better.'

'Well…if you're sure. Just for a bit.'

Dusk faded slowly enough for that bit of time

to stretch. They worked until it was too dark to really see the stone being uncovered and then carried on, being guided by the sound of their tools scraping the solid stone.

David had rolled his trousers up but his shirt was streaked with mud and his shoes would never be the same.

'Look at you,' Anne said laughingly at last. 'You're absolutely filthy.'

David nodded ruefully. 'And I'm starving.'

'Me too.'

David jammed the spade into the impressive mound of earth they'd created. He looked at the shadowy outline of the old pond they'd revealed. 'Whose silly idea was this?'

'Yours.' Anne was still smiling. 'And it wasn't silly. I love it.' She stepped up from the spot that had had the most earth cleared and David held his hand out to take her spade.

Why didn't she let it go?

If she had, she wouldn't have been pulled so close to this mud-streaked, dishevelled, sweaty, *happy* man. She wouldn't have been inside that bubble again and it wouldn't have had the chance to shrink around them like a skin, moulding them into one entity.

A tangle of limbs and hands and lips. An almost desperate fumbling that only stilled when David's lips found hers and Anne could abandon any rational thought and simply fall into the kiss.

It wasn't enough. Not this time. And they both knew it. When David eased back and took her hand and began to lead her towards the house, Anne was more than willing to follow him.

'We need a shower,' he told her. 'We're very dirty.'

'Mmm.' They both knew they weren't going to be using separate showers. It was just as well Anne was as fit as she was, she decided, otherwise her legs couldn't possibly have kept her upright and walking in step with David. Not when everything inside seemed to be turning into the most delicious liquid imaginable.

This wasn't simply about sex.

As much as David wanted—no, *needed*—to

make love to Anne, he knew that physical intimacy was only part of a much bigger picture.

And if he hadn't realised that as he led her into his house and up the stairs to his newly renovated en suite bathroom, he knew it as soon as he'd finished undressing Anne and taken her into the tiled shower with its multiple jets that surrounded them both.

Rivulets of muddy water trickled away from a body that had changed surprisingly little after the pregnancy. Her breasts were a little larger maybe and her stomach was still soft and generous, but when David soaped his hands and drew her closer to clean off the remaining dirt, her skin still felt like silk. The curves were familiar and delicious. He crouched to rub the engrained mud from her knees, loving the feel of her body beneath his hands but knowing that caring for her like this—making her clean and, later on, feeding her—was just as compelling as any physical fulfillment that could be on the agenda.

Maybe this was a mistake but he was lost in

the wonder of being here at all. Being with Anne. Being allowed to care for and touch the woman he loved.

Would always love.

Anne tipped her head back, feeling the warmth of the water on her neck and back and the delicious slide of soapy hands on her skin. It should have been embarrassing having her muddy knees rubbed clean, but David's hands were moving upwards now. Caressing her inner thighs. Slipping behind to cradle her bottom as he stood up and pulled her closer.

His lips felt cool in comparison to the warmth of the shower but they still burned wherever they touched, just like his hands did. On her breasts and neck and mouth. Anne had been trying to return the favour of being washed but the sponge that foamed with shower gel slipped from her hands in the end. She needed everything she had to cling to David and stay upright.

'I want you,' he said simply, his mouth moving against hers.

'I want you, too.'

'It's too soon, isn't it?'

'I don't think so.' She could feel the hardness that was David wanting her, pressing against her. 'No, I'm sure it isn't.' She pressed back, desire so urgent it was unbearable.

David groaned, lifting her. Easing her back so that she was supported against tiles warmed by the rain still falling around and over them.

He was being cautious. Careful. It was Anne's turn to groan then. She wrapped her legs around him and begged for more, hanging on for dear life as her words unleashed the kind of passion she remembered so well. A kind she knew she would never find with anyone else.

It was blinding. A lightning bolt that was over too fast for either of them. So David wrapped them both in fluffy towels and took her to his bed and this time they made love slowly and gently. Retracing maps they both knew but wanted to rediscover in exquisite detail. This time David produced protection, even though Anne was sure she hadn't started ovulating again yet and was at no risk of pregnancy.

'Better safe than sorry,' David murmured.

A tiny comment soon lost in pleasure of each other's bodies but it surfaced again later, as Anne lay in David's arms and let him decide what food he was going to have delivered to the house as soon as possible.

Would she be sorry if she found she was pregnant with David's child?

If only she could answer that question. Because if she could, she wouldn't be feeling so lost right now.

As though she was standing at a crossroads, knowing that the next steps she took would determine the direction she would have to take for the rest of her life. But she was lost and couldn't find anything that resembled a compass.

She wasn't alone.

David was here at the same crossroads. Was history going to repeat itself and have them choose different directions or was it possible that their hands and hearts could stay linked as they moved forward?

Only one thing seemed certain. The time allowed to stay at the crossroads was limited.

And the clock had already been ticking for weeks now.

CHAPTER EIGHT

Choices.

They could be both a blessing and a curse.

'I had no idea goldfish came in so many colours.'

'Neither did I.' David bent down to peer into the tank in front of Anne. There was a huge variety of fish suitable for a garden pond. Big ones, little ones, shiny and speckled. The colours ranged from fluorescent orange and yellow to a deep red. Brown, even.

'How on earth are you going to choose?'

'That's why I dragged you along. Look, even the fins are different shapes. That one's all frilly. Must be a girl fish.'

The pet shop salesgirl, busy with a nearby tank, smiled as she overheard the exchange.

'It's your pond,' Anne told him. 'You get to choose.'

'There wouldn't be a pond if it wasn't for you. *You* choose.'

Anne turned her head, caught by something in David's tone. A note that suggested this was about more than fish. Not that the salesgirl would have picked up on it but, then, she knew nothing of their history.

Or how things had changed in the last couple of weeks since they had begun sharing a bed again. A choice had been made then too but so far neither seemed to be ready to really talk about the implications of what was happening. If they did, more choices would have to be made and there was a very real risk of their rediscovered intimacy vanishing in a puff of smoke that would leave them both burned.

Was that what was underlying David's insistence that she make the choice about the fish? Because the time was coming when she would have to make a rather more personal choice? A choice that was so huge it was terrifying.

To be with David or to be alone.

To be a mother or to continue the career she loved unchecked.

A flash of panic made her break the eye contact with him. Anne stared into the tank again but she wasn't seeing a single fish.

Why was she so afraid? That she would make the wrong choice? Or that she couldn't make it at all? Given how much she knew she loved this man, that choice should have been easy. She loved the way he looked. Her heart skipped a beat every time she saw him when they'd been apart for a while. She loved the sound of his voice. His smile. His dedication to his job and his ability to do it so well. Most of all, she loved the way he cared about *her*. Even now, when she was feeling so fit and well again, he still kept an eye on how much rest she was getting and that she was eating good food. She knew that if she wobbled in any way, he would be ready to scoop her into his arms and make sure she would be all right.

What woman in her right mind would let

someone who cared about her like that leave their life? The choice should be a no-brainer. She could choose to be a mother and give David the family he wanted so badly and that would be enough to keep them together, quite probably for ever.

Except it wouldn't be enough, would it?

Why not? Was her career that important to her? And if it was, why had she made life so tough for herself over the last year by having babies for Julia and Mac?

The fish swam happily amongst the oxygen weed and rocks but still Anne couldn't focus.

Love… That was why she'd tipped her life upside down and had those babies. Real, unconditional, forever kind of love. The kind she had for Jules. The kind Julia and Mac had for each other.

Mac had wanted a family. Julia had known she couldn't give it to him and had taken herself away to give him the chance to have that family with someone else. Mac had crossed the world to find her again because being with Jules was more important. It had been his love for her that had been more important than anything else.

Did David feel that way about her? If he did, then anything would be possible. The memory of the way he had carried her in his arms to safety that day by the river was enough to make her believe he might but if he did, why was it *her* that had to make a choice?

She didn't want to. She didn't want to risk losing what they had. Even if it was only for a few more weeks, she couldn't bring herself to pre-empt whatever was coming.

'I can't choose,' she said aloud, finally. Oh, Lord, was there a note of desperation in her voice? 'It's a big pond. Can't you take some of each colour?'

David gave a huff of laughter. 'That's so like you, Annie. All or nothing.' He turned away from the tank. 'Maybe I'd better get you out of here before you start looking at the kittens.'

'How's the work on the house going, David?'

'Almost done, thank goodness.' In a rare lull

in emergency department activity, David had found time to not only eat his lunch but to be enjoying a cup of surprisingly good coffee from the espresso machine in the staffroom.

'Looking good?'

'Amazing. It's exceeded all expectations.' He smiled at the registrar and she smiled back, the eye contact lingering just long enough for David to get the message before she turned to use the coffee machine.

The young doctor was pretty. He knew she was good at her job. He also knew she was doing her emergency department rotation as part of her general practitioner training. She was heading for a career as a family doctor so it could be part time when she might have her own family to factor into her life.

That should have been enough on its own to have made her a blip on David's radar, never mind the fact that she was clever and attractive. He searched hopefully in that instant of eye contact but a heartbeat was as long as it took.

No blip. Not even a glimmer of one. He had absolutely no interest in this woman.

Dammit!

What was it about Anne Bennett that eclipsed other women to such a degree they couldn't even glimmer, let alone shine?

A woman who couldn't even compromise on the colour of fish, let alone juggle the idea of a career *and* a family. So black and white. All or nothing.

It was ridiculous. Couldn't she see that she was shooting herself in the foot as far as a meaningful relationship went? He *loved* her, for God's sake. She was shooting them *both* in the foot. David frowned at his coffee as a disturbing thought occurred to him. Was he guilty of the same sin?

He'd been prepared to walk away from Anne once before because he couldn't have it all. He'd left himself with nothing, hadn't he? Well, he'd still had his career, of course, but had that been enough?

'So...' The registrar sat down at the table opposite David. 'You'll be going on the market soon, then?'

'Sorry?' Good grief, was she asking if he was planning to be available for a new relationship?

She raised her eyebrows. 'The house? With it being finished? Wasn't that the plan?'

'Oh…yes.' It had indeed been the plan.

The house was finished. So was the garden, right down to the pond with its baby waterlilies and a rainbow of fish. Anne's cottage was finished, too. She was going there this afternoon, in fact, to check on the final touches. David had asked her to walk there via the hospital so he could come and see it as well. He was due to finish at 3 p.m. and a leisurely stroll home would be nice.

He wanted to see the cottage. Not to make sure that the workmen had done a good job but because he wanted to see whether he could pick up any vibes that maybe Anne wasn't so excited at the thought of moving back to her own home.

That maybe she would rather stay where she was.

With him.

'I'm not sure,' he said aloud into the silence. 'About selling the house.'

'But aren't you due to leave soon? You've got that flash job in London to go to, haven't you?' The young doctor's eyes were shining. 'I'd *love* to go and work in London. It would *so* exciting.'

'Mmm.' David smiled back in an attempt to catch some of the excitement his junior colleague was emanating.

It should be exciting. All of it. That the house and garden were looking fabulous enough to command a quick, easy sale at a top price. That he had a prestigious position waiting for him in a world-renowned hospital in the one of the most wonderful cities on the globe.

And…he didn't want to go.

He'd been given a choice only that morning. They wanted him to stay on here, in a senior consultancy position. Only a step away from Head of Department and they'd intimated that taking that step would only be a matter of time.

His best intentions—the ones he'd had when he'd come back here—to tie up loose ends and move on with his life had been derailed. He only had himself to blame but there it was. Those intentions hung on one end of a balance and the rekindled romance with Anne hung on the other end.

Where was Anne?

Right in the middle. Depending on which way she moved, the balance would shift and the choice would be easy. Or, if not easy, at least clear.

Maybe he was standing there in the middle as well. Right beside her. He had his own choices that he could make and therefore influence the balance himself. He could decide that being with Anne was more important than having a child.

It *was* more important. There was a principle here that was far bigger than making babies. It was to do with the whole feeling of family. Of loving someone enough for what they wanted or needed to be more important than what you wanted yourself. Was the fact that he and Anne had been pulling in directions different enough to have snapped their relationship once already enough evidence that the kind of love they had wasn't a lasting kind?

He simply didn't know. He desperately wanted to find out and that was what the last weeks with Anne had been about. They were closer than they'd ever been in so many ways but he didn't feel any closer to knowing the answer to what the future held.

Choices still had to be made. And soon.

Just before 3 p.m. the quiet spell in the emergency department ended dramatically with the arrival of first one and then another ambulance coming from the scene of a multi-vehicle pile-up on the motorway. The trauma bays were already full and every available staff member occupied with the assessment and treatment of the injured people when a third ambulance pulled into the loading bay. Arriving right behind the stretcher that was unloaded from the vehicle was Anne.

'Status 1,' the paramedic confirmed the call that had prompted David and a senior nurse to be waiting out here to meet them. 'Ten-year-old boy who was thrown from a car and then trapped when the vehicle rolled. Chest injuries. Increasing respiratory difficulty. Query pneumothorax.'

'Check Resus 1,' David instructed the nurse. 'Make sure that patient is on the way to CT and the area is clear.'

This little boy was clearly not stable. The tendons on his neck were standing out in his struggle to breathe and the trace on the ECG monitor sitting on the end of the stretcher was showing a sprinkling of abnormal heartbeats.

'Need a hand?'

David was reaching to push the button to open the automatic doors. Thinking ahead to what he would need around him in the next few minutes when they'd transferred this child to the bed in the well-equipped resuscitation area. A chest drain kit, intubation gear, bag mask, X-rays. A central line maybe.

He blinked at Anne as the doors slid open in the wake of her offer to assist.

Was it because she'd been away from work and so engrossed in projects that had nothing to do with medicine that he hadn't made such an instant, obvious connection?

This child was critically ill with major chest trauma.

Dr Anne Bennett was a specialist paediatric cardiothoracic surgeon. The best possible person to take over this case.

'Sure.' This was definitely a no-brainer. This was what Anne did. Who she was. Why did this action of stepping back to let her take over give him the briefest flash of something that felt like…disappointment?

The patient who had been occupying the resus area they were heading for was being wheeled out as they came in but the woman was conscious and cried out as she saw the small figure on the stretcher.

'*Daniel!* Is he…? Will he be…?' Her words became choked by sobs and she covered her face with her hands. 'Oh… *God…*'

David stepped closer to the departing bed. 'We're going to take the best care of him that we can,' he assured the woman, who was presumably Daniel's mother. 'Try not to worry. He's lucky that he's got the best specialist available right here.'

'On the count of three,' Anne was saying, ahead of him now and pulling a paper gown over her clothing as she spoke. 'One…two…three.'

The small body was lifted to the bed and remnants of clothing cut clear. One doctor was in charge of the airway and had an ambu-bag hooked onto the overhead oxygen supply, ready to cover the boy's face and try and squeeze oxygen into his lungs.

'Saturation's right down.' A nurse checked the clips over one of Daniel's fingers. 'Eighty per cent and dropping.'

'Blood pressure's dropping too,' came another

voice as new figures appeared on the bank of monitors. 'Systolic down to 93.'

'Run of V tach,' someone else warned as an alarm on the cardiac monitor sounded. 'Okay, back into sinus.'

Anne unhooked her stethoscope from her ears. 'Flail chest,' she reported. 'No breath sounds on the left side. I need a chest drain kit, please.'

The sterile kit was unrolled onto a trolley by the time she had pulled gloves on.

'Check his belly, could you, please, David? And his pelvis. He's losing a lot of blood.'

'I'll get some more fluids up as well and get him cross-matched for some whole blood.'

Anne nodded, now intent on the task of inserting a tube between small ribs to release the air and blood now trapped in the chest cavity and making it impossible for normal breathing. A task made harder by the crush injury that had left so many ribs shattered.

'V tach again,' came the warning as Anne swabbed the boy's chest with disinfectant and

was paused with a scalpel in her hand. 'No...
V fib... He's arrested.'

'Stand clear.' Anne reached for the life-pack
controls. 'Shocking now.'

She watched the screen intently as a normal
rhythm emerged from the straight line following
the shock. Then she looked up as a newcomer
entered a now crowded space. David could sense
her relief to see the anaesthetist she probably
worked with on a regular basis.

'Good to see you, Bob. This lad needs tubing.
I think we're looking at doing a thoracotamy.'

'Tamponade?

'Looks like it.'

David agreed silently. There was so much
bleeding going on in that small chest that it was
becoming impossible for the heart to work normally, let alone the lungs. Having checked and
found no obvious injuries to the boy's abdomen
or pelvis, he was beginning to feel redundant.
Daniel's legs and head also seem to have escaped major trauma. It was the chest that had

caught the brunt of whatever had trapped this child in the wreckage.

He could—and probably should—go and check the other patients who had come in from this scene but he knew they were well attended by staff who would come and get him if he was needed. And none of them had been anywhere near as critically injured as this young child.

And this was compelling drama. Opening someone's chest in an emergency department was fortunately a rare occurrence. If it had to happen—as was becoming evident it was in this case—because the patient wouldn't survive long enough to get to Theatre without it, then you couldn't hope for anyone better than a surgeon who specialised in doing exactly this kind of procedure.

That so many people were watching and hanging off every movement and word that came from Anne was clearly not fazing her at all.

She had that kind of intense focus that made anything other than the life she was trying to save totally irrelevant. The way she had been that first day David had seen her when he'd come back here. With the backdrop of another case of child chest trauma. Another little life that she'd had the ability to save. Who the hell did he think he was to even consider himself worth compromising such a brilliant career for?

He had the weird feeling that a circle was closing. That something was very close to being complete.

Over.

'Clamp, thanks.' Somehow, amongst the terrible open wound that was this little boy's chest now, Anne had found something that made her tone triumphant. 'Laceration of the left ventricle,' she told her audience. 'I'll put in a temporary suture and we'll get him straight up to Theatre. How's the BP now?'

'Coming up. Systolic 95.'

'Oxygen saturation?'

'Improving. Eight-six per cent and rising.'

'Good.' Anne's hands were making swift, graceful movements, the thread of the suture invisible from where David was standing. She glanced in his direction. 'David, could you alert Theatre that we'll be on the way up in less than five minutes, please?'

'Sure.' Was she intending to go into Theatre with Daniel?

As if reading her thoughts, Anne spoke again. 'Page Jeff, too. If he's not available, I'll scrub. We don't want to lose any time.'

David had waited for her.

It was nearly 6 p.m. by the time Anne left the paediatric intensive care unit but she found him in his office when she walked past on her way to leave the hospital.

'I thought you might have gone home.'

'I was waiting for you. We had plans, remember?'

He didn't look happy. Why? Because she'd stepped in and taken over a major case in his department?

'Daniel's looking okay,' she told him. 'He'll be on a ventilator for a while but he's oxygenating well and his cardiac function's looking stable. He's got a fighting chance.'

'Lucky for him that you arrived when you did.'

'You could have done it,' Anne said quietly. 'But I'm glad I was there. It was…'

What she'd been missing even though she hadn't realised she was missing it. That adrenaline rush. The amazing zone where you could put every ounce of your skill into making sure no tiny detail got missed. The kind of case that was so unlikely to be successful but when it was…

'It was amazing,' she said aloud. 'Don't you love it when you win against odds like that?'

'Absolutely.' But David's smile looked strained. 'Shall we go? Do you still want to drop in at the cottage?'

Anne was still watching his face. Looking for clues that might explain this odd tension in the room. She had no idea why but she was quite sure that going to the cottage with him would make it worse.

'Not really,' she said cautiously.

'Of course.' David was shutting down his computer. 'You'll want to hang around for a while. In case you're needed for any follow-up on the boy.'

'The boy'? David knew Daniel's name. He was deliberately trying to make this less personal. More professional. To do with the job, not the people involved, as if it was possible to separate them.

The penny dropped and Anne knew what this new tension was all about. No wonder the prospect of going to her old home in David's company had rung alarm bells. That cottage had been the scene of the final unravelling of their relationship. The arguments.

His plans had been unexpectedly disrupted this afternoon and old buttons had been pushed. The ones created by interrupted dates or the inability to leave town for a romantic weekend away. He'd been left by himself. Waiting for her. Anne could almost hear the echo of angry voices in the back of her mind.

'Nothing matters more than your career, Anne. You're selfish.'

'That's the pot calling the kettle black, isn't it? You want me to sacrifice my career to have children. That's worse than selfish. Positively Victorian.'

'If love is involved, it's called compromise, not sacrifice. But you don't know that word, do you? Not the meaning of it, anyway.'

Anne could almost feel the same anger she'd felt then at being accused of being selfish. She'd never been selfish. She'd given up a normal childhood and teenage years to be a mother. She'd given the use of her body to her sister to create a family for her.

Did David still think she was being selfish? Just because she'd become so involved in this afternoon's case that she'd missed a kind of date with him?

No. Of course he wouldn't be that petty. Maybe the combination of circumstances had given him the kind of flashback she'd just experienced. She was probably looking less than happy herself right at this moment.

'I don't need to stay here,' she said quietly. 'But I have left my mobile number and asked to be called if there are any concerns with Daniel during this post-operative phase.' Her tone rose a little defensively. 'He's become my patient, David. You didn't have to hand him over to me, you know.'

'Oh, but I did.' David was on his feet, coming out from behind his desk. 'A life was at stake, Annie. I would have doing less than my job if I hadn't provided the best care I possibly could.' He put his hands on Anne's shoulders, bent down and kissed her lips gently. 'That was you. The best. I'm not at all convinced that young Daniel would have even made it to Theatre if you hadn't been there. I'm proud of you.'

He sounded sincere. He had used the softened version of her name that only the people closest to her ever used. His kiss had been real. The glow of pleasure lasted until Anne pulled back far enough to meet his gaze but then it spluttered and died. There was something in his eyes that scared her.

Something that reminded her of what she'd seen—or rather, heard—not so long ago. When he'd been talking about the pond. Something beautiful that had been lost. Did he think that he'd lost her? That the pull of her amazing career was something he couldn't—or didn't want—to compete with?

The choice loomed closer. Maybe this was as good a time as any to talk about it. Anne drew in a deep breath and gathered her courage but just as she opened her mouth to speak, the mobile phone in her bag began to trill.

'Daniel?'

'No.' Anne had fished the phone from its pocket and frowned at the screen. 'It's Jules. On her mobile.'

She answered the call but, for several seconds, she could make no sense of what she was hearing. Her sister sounded hysterical. There were babies crying and a loud, mechanical kind of noise. There even seemed to be a siren going nearby.

'Calm down,' she instructed Julia. 'I don't understand. Take a deep breath and start again, hon. Where are you? What's all the noise about?'

She listened carefully. She asked a couple of questions and heard herself automatically saying reassuring things. Then she ended the call and looked at David.

'*What?*' he demanded.

'Oh, my God...' Anne wanted to close her eyes and make this all go away but she couldn't. She clung to David's gaze and tried to get the words from a throat that suddenly felt too tight to breathe, let alone speak.

'What is it?' David said. He was holding her, with both his gaze and his tone. Steadily. 'Tell me.'

Anne swallowed. Hard. She could feel the prickle of tears in her eyes and her voice could only emerge in a whisper.

'Mac's helicopter has crashed.'

CHAPTER NINE

HIS arms were around her in an instant.

Holding her close.

Giving her that same sense of safety they always did. Advertising David's ability to care for *her*. And, yes, it was other people Anne had to worry about right now. Mac, of course—her dearly beloved brother-in-law. Julia, not only at this point but possibly for the rest of her life, if the worst had happened and she had lost the man she loved so much. And there were two tiny babies, who might have lost their father.

David cared about these people too but his first action was to look after *her*. To be the rock from which she could gather the strength she would need to face this crisis.

How could she ever survive without this in her life?

She couldn't. That was all there was to it but this wasn't the time to be thinking about herself or how she could secure the future she knew she needed. Or imagining how she would feel if her fear had been for David's life and not Mac's. It crept in, though, just for a heartbeat. Long enough for her to know that she loved this man quite probably just as much as Julia loved Mac.

The murmurs of sympathy and encouragement were filtering into the panicked buzzing in Anne's head. Becoming words. Instructions.

'We need to go,' David was saying. 'I'll take you to Jules.'

'No.' Anne shook her head, feeling the solid wall of David's chest against her forehead. Taking in a deep breath that filled her with the warmth and scent of him because she couldn't know how long it might be before she could be this close again. 'She's coming here.'

'What? She's not driving?'

'No.' Anne scrubbed at her face. The tears had gone and she felt calm now. Ready to do whatever needed to be done. 'The news of the crash came through Ambulance Control. Jules has her best friends in the service. They weren't about to let a police officer she'd never met arrive on her doorstep with that news. They dispatched a free ambulance crew.'

'But they're coming here? To Emergency?'

Anne nodded.

David looked pale. 'Why? Is someone hurt? Jules? One of the babies?'

'No.' Anne had to touch him. To find a smile. To offer him just a fraction of what he'd been able to give her. Reassurance. Strength. 'They asked Jules what she needed and she said…' Anne had to take a breath to fight the wobble in her voice. 'She said she needed me.'

'And you said you were here.'

'Yes. We can take her home but maybe this is a better place to be. They haven't found the helicopter yet but when they do… If Mac's injured and not…' Anne had to press her lips together to stop any more words coming out. She had to close her eyes to try not to see the worst.

'If he's injured they might bring him here,'

David finished for her. 'Yes. That makes sense. All right, let's go and see if the relatives' room is free. Otherwise we can find another space that will be private.'

He took hold of Anne's hand and led her from the office. Word in the department spread like wildfire and the availability of the relatives' room was guaranteed. When the ambulance pulled into the loading bay a short time later they were both standing there, waiting for the back doors to open.

Julia stumbled out first and almost fell into her sister's arms. It was David who gripped the handles of the two baby car seats and carried the infants inside. Bags that had clearly been hastily stuffed with things the twins might need were carried in by a paramedic who followed the small procession, oblivious to curious stares, as it made its way through the emergency department and into the room set aside for them.

'Thank you so much,' Julia said to the bag carrier. 'I don't know what I would have done if you hadn't been the one to come and tell me.'

'No worries,' the paramedic assured her, giving her a hug. 'Is there anything else I can do?'

Julia shook her head. 'You guys need to get back on the road and I'm okay. I've got Annie now. Just…can you get someone to tell me any news? You might hear something that…that they might wait to tell me.'

The paramedic nodded, his face grim. 'They've sent a search and rescue spotter plane out. If the emergency beacon's working we should hear something soon. One of us will call it through.'

Anne had her arm around her sister again. 'Let me give you my mobile number. And a landline in case we decide to go home.'

It wasn't until she'd recited the numbers and the paramedic was leaving that Anne realised she had automatically given the landline number of David's house as her home.

Because, in the space of the last few weeks, it had become her home, hadn't it?

Where her heart was.

Had David noticed? Turning, Anne saw that he

was crouched beside one of the car seats, undoing the safety belt to release one of the crying babies.

Julia had moved to crouch beside the other seat. 'They're hungry,' she was telling David. 'And probably wet.'

'No problem,' David said calmly. 'We'll get them sorted in no time, don't you worry.'

The noise level was escalating. Angus and Amy seemed to think that being taken from the cocoon of their car seats was yet another tribulation. They were both red-faced and howling. Tiny fists punched the air to underline their misery.

This was a nightmare.

Julia needed comfort. Support. A calm environment would help. What would it be like to be faced with the sense of being unable to cope with the background horror that she might have to parent alone for ever?

Anne started digging in the bags. Looking for nappies and wipes. Formula and bottles and dry clothes.

'Maybe we need some help,' she said. 'I could find a nurse who's not busy, maybe.'

David and Julia both looked at her. Julia looked bemused, as though she didn't quite understand what Anne meant. Weirdly, Anne thought she saw that odd note of sadness in David's expression again.

'We're fine, Annie,' he said gently. 'This is about family. We don't need anyone else.'

He was holding Amy in his arms now. He lifted the baby so that she was pressed against his chest. Close to his heartbeat, as Anne had been herself so recently. The tiny head with its fluffy, dark hair and that endearing bald spot on the back was nestled against David's neck.

Unsurprisingly, the baby's howls started to diminish.

'There you go.' David smiled, turning his head so that his lips brushed Amy's head. 'That's better, isn't it, princess?'

Anne swallowed what felt like a hard lump in her throat. He was right. This was about family. Staying close and looking after each other. Had he seen her offer to find extra help as an admission of failure, perhaps? Did he think that she was trying to avoid dealing with this herself because of some personal issues stemming from the surrogacy? Or, worse, that she was simply being *selfish*?

'Let me take Angus for you,' she said to Julia.

'Maybe you could make up some formula.' Julia was bouncing Angus gently in her arms. 'Have you found the tin? And the bottles?'

Anne nodded. 'There's a microwave in the staffroom. Or do I need to boil some water? And how many scoops for each bottle?'

'I'd better do it,' Julia decided. 'Here, you take Gus. I know where everything is.'

'I'll come with you.'

'No. They get more upset if they're separated. I'm okay, Annie.' Julia was pale and her eyes huge and dark but her voice was steady. She carefully transferred her noisy bundle into her sister's arms.

'Are you sure?'

Julia smiled. 'I probably know my way around here better than you do. It's part of where I worked, remember? And it's…part of where Mac works. I feel closer to him here and…it'll help if I have something to do.'

Anne was blinking back tears. Good grief, she was supposed to be the strong one. How come she hadn't noticed her baby sister turning into such a strong woman? She felt completely out of her depth here. She should be taking charge and giving Julia strength, not the other way around. This was confusing at some level. Or maybe it was because she was being handed the responsibility of her nephew and she wasn't sure she was ready for this yet.

Ready or not, she had no choice.

Poor Anne.

She was rocking Angus in her arms, walking round and round the only available space between the couches in this room, looking less and less sure of herself.

'What am I doing wrong?' she asked David.

'Nothing, love. He's sad because he's hungry. And probably because he's got wet pants.'

'Okay. I can deal with that.'

'Sure you can. You're way ahead of me in baby skills.'

Anne knelt on the floor, carefully adjusting her burden so that she could use one hand to sort through one of the bags.

'It's more than a quarter of a century since I changed a nappy,' she said. 'And we used cloth ones, not disposables.' She laid a towel on the floor and put Angus down to unbutton his suit.

'Phew!' She screwed up her nose a moment later. 'Some things don't change. I might need a bathtub here.'

David grinned. 'Wipes should do it. They'll be in that bag there somewhere.'

Anne's face was a picture as she held the baby's feet in the air and started to wipe a small dirty bottom. Her movements were tentative at first and Angus obviously realised that he was in the hands of someone who might not know what they were doing. His shrieks reached an impressive decibel level.

'Want to swap?' he offered.

'No.' Anne sounded as though her teeth were gritted. 'I can do this.'

Of course she could but it was impossible not to compare this Anne to the woman he'd seen in Resus 1 a few hours ago. That intently focused, brilliant surgeon. She'd been doing what she was meant to be doing then. What she wanted to do. Looking skilled and competent.

Now she was looking lost and miserable. She had to be worried sick about Mac. And Julia. And maybe she hadn't been ready to get this involved with the babies she'd given birth to but wasn't going to parent. And maybe there was another fear that she might not have even acknowledged yet. If the worst had happened and Mac wasn't coming home then she would, by default, become a second parent to her nephew and niece because there was no way she would leave Julia to face the future alone.

Ironic in a way. He'd realised today that he

could never ask Anne to compromise her career for the sake of family but fate might be forcing her to do just that.

With children that weren't hers. Or his.

Unconsciously, David tightened his grip on the baby he held. They needed protection, these precious babies. He wouldn't allow himself to think of the worst case scenario.

'You're doing great,' he told Anne, who was reaching for a clean nappy now.

'Which bit goes at the front?'

'I think it's the bit with the sticky tabs. No... maybe it's the other way round.' Good grief, neither of them was exactly qualified to be doing this, were they?

Julia arrived back with two warm bottles of formula as Anne was struggling to keep small, chubby legs still for long enough to stick the nappy in place. She caught David's gaze and her eyebrows rose in a silent query about whether Anne was coping. He smiled.

'Sit down,' he suggested. 'And take Amy. She

needs her mum. Give me the other bottle and I'll rescue Annie.'

Anne had picked Angus up. The buttons on his stretch suit were gaping in a peculiar fashion and having a clean bottom hadn't made him any happier. Anne looked over to where Julia was sitting with Amy, who had taken to her bottle, and then she looked at David and he could see despair in her face.

'I'll take him,' he said. 'You need to wash your hands.'

By the time she returned, David was sitting the couch beside Julia and Angus lay in his arms, sucking furiously on his bottle, wide eyes staring up at the unfamiliar man who was feeding him. The only sound in the room was the contented sucking noises the babies were making.

Until Anne's phone rang.

Julia flinched and then froze, watching as Anne took the call.

'They're within range of the beacon,' she relayed moments later.

'Radio contact?' David queried.

Anne shook her head. 'But there's hours of daylight left. They'll find them soon.'

The wait seemed interminable. Having been fed and changed and cuddled, the twins settled to sleep in the cushioned comfort of their car seats, a fuzzy blanket draped over them for warmth. David sat on a couch with a hand on each handle, rocking the seats gently. Anne held Julia in her arms on the other couch. A silent support that spoke of a bond too deep to measure.

And then someone knocked on the door.

'Jules?' It was the same paramedic who had brought her here. 'They've found them.'

David watched the sisters straighten. They both had the same frozen expression on their faces. They were holding each other's hands so tightly it had to hurt.

'They're alive,' the paramedic said. 'Both of them. The radio gear's been knocked out of action but the chopper is pretty well intact and they're both on safe ground. In bush country, so the plane couldn't land.'

'Oh...' For the first time since she'd arrived at

the hospital, Julia burst into tears. 'Oh… Thank goodness!'

'They're not hurt?' Anne whispered.

'Not badly, from what could be seen. Mac was lying on the ground but he was waving, apparently. They reckoned he had a big grin on his face.'

Julia hiccupped and smiled. 'That's my Mac.'

'They're sending a chopper. It's about thirty minutes' flight time and I'm on the crew to go. I came to see if you wanted to come with us, Jules.'

'Oh…' Julia sprang to her feet. *'Yes.'*

But then she looked at her babies, asleep in their seats. Her gaze lifted to meet David's and the plea was as eloquent as her turmoil. She didn't want to leave the babies but she had to go to Mac. He was the love of her life and she'd been terrified she might lose him.

And a part of David's heart broke because he knew exactly how she felt. It was the way he would feel about Anne. They way he would want someone to feel about him. That he was *that* important.

No. Not someone.

Only Anne.

'Go.' David smiled at Julia. 'We'll look after these two, won't we, Annie?'

Anne nodded. She had tears on her cheeks and she got up to give Julia one last, swift hug. 'Go and bring him home,' she said brokenly. 'His family's waiting for him.'

David was so good with the babies.

When Angus woke and grizzled, he soothed him with rocking and soft words. When Amy woke and didn't settle, he picked her up and cuddled her. She fell asleep in his arms and he sat very still on the couch, not wanting to disturb her.

He looked tired. His tie had been abandoned a while ago and his shirtsleeves were rolled up. His hair was tousled and his jaw deeply shadowed. Anne couldn't help remembering the day he'd walked across the lawn towards

her, looking a bit like this. The day they'd discovered the lost pond. And each other again.

This situation couldn't be more different. It
had nothing to do with sex or even herself and
David as a couple. This was a bigger picture. A
family picture but, curiously, the bond between
them seemed stronger. So powerful it took her
breath away and blurred her vision.

Or was that exhaustion kicking in, in the wake
of that tense stint in Theatre and then the stress
of being so afraid for Mac and his brand-new
family? They still didn't know how badly he
might be injured. There'd been some delay in
getting another chopper off the ground. The
rescue team might be lucky to get to the scene
before daylight faded completely at this rate.

'We should go home,' David said into the
silence of the room. 'That way we could get
something to eat and have a rest ourselves. We
could be in for a long night.'

'Mmm.' It was a sensible suggestion. They
could get back to the hospital quickly enough if
they needed to.

But she was reluctant to move. This picture of him sitting there with Amy in his arms was compelling. And confusing. She wanted David to want her as more than a mother for his children but his life wasn't going to be complete without his own family, was it?

He was right. Taking a stand about having children of her own had been selfish. How lucky would that child—or children—be to have a father like him? She already knew how lucky she would be to have him caring for her. Protecting her.

Loving her.

'David?'

He looked up. But his gaze kept travelling when a nurse poked her head through the door. 'Dr Bennett?'

Anne's head turned swiftly. 'Yes?'

'Word is that they're on scene. Mac has a compound fracture of his ankle but is otherwise okay. It'll be an hour or more before they get back and it sounds like he'll be going to Theatre as soon as possible after that.' The nurse hesitated. 'Are you and Dr Earnshaw planning to stay in here?'

'You need the room?'

The nurse bit her lip. 'We've got a man who's terminal. His family's having to take turns to sit with him and they're not getting much privacy in the waiting room.'

'We were thinking of taking the twins home,' David said. 'Maybe you could order a taxi for us?'

David got Amy buckled back into her car seat while Anne packed up all their belongings.

'Are you sure you don't mind?' she asked David. 'You have to walk tomorrow. I could take them back to the cottage.'

'I think they need both of us to get settled at least,' David said. 'Then you'll be able to come back to be with Jules.'

Anne nodded, relieved. She certainly couldn't manage this without David's help. She was zipping up the second bag of baby gear when her mobile phone rang again.

'Maybe it's Jules,' she said hopefully.

It wasn't.

The call was from a registrar in the paediatric intensive care unit. Daniel's blood pressure was dropping. His ECG trace was becoming erratic and his lung function causing concern.

'I'm on my way,' Anne had to say.

And then she looked at where David was standing, holding a car seat in each hand.

'Daniel's in trouble,' she told him. 'I'll have to go and see him. Could we take the twins up to the relatives' room up there?'

'What's going to happen if Daniel needs to go back to Theatre?'

Anne swallowed. Hard. 'I'll have to take him.'

David's face was grim. 'If I'm going to be babysitting for hours by myself, I'd rather be doing it in my own house.'

Anne stared at him. This couldn't be happening. When that nurse had come into this room, she'd been on the point of telling David that she wanted to be with him for ever. That she wanted to have a family with him. But this was exactly what she'd feared all along, wasn't it?

The conflict between her career and family. The last thing in the world she wanted right now was to leave David to look after the babies by himself. Or to be unavailable when Julia had to sit and wait for Mac to come out of Theatre.

The pull of family was overwhelming.

The pull of duty unavoidable. A life was at stake. Someone else's child.

Conflict. Career versus family and child care.

A sound that could almost have been a huff of ironic laughter escaped her lips. She'd been running from making this choice but here it was, right in front of her and, in the end, no matter how agonising it was, she didn't actually have a choice at all.

'I have to go and see Daniel. He's my patient.'

'Of course you do.'

'Will you be all right? With…the babies?'

'Yes.'

'I'm…so sorry, David.'

He grunted an acceptance of her apology but his face was bleak. 'So am I.'

They stared at each other. Echoes of the past whispered around them and stung like an icy breeze.

'It was never going to work, was it?' Anne asked softly.

They both knew what she was talking about.

'No,' David agreed sadly. 'I guess it wasn't.'

CHAPTER TEN

THAT simple exchange had sounded the death knell of their relationship.

It was still ringing in Anne's ears hours later when she accompanied Julia back to David's house to collect the babies.

And her things.

'So…' David was standing in the entrance hall when she came out of the guest suite with her suitcase. 'You're leaving, then.'

It wasn't a question but Anne nodded. 'I need to go home with Jules. She needs me.'

The silence was deafening. What had she hoped she would hear? David saying that *he* needed her, too?

'She tells me Mac's doing well.' His voice was tight.

'We waited until he came round from the anaesthetic. They've done an amazing job of putting his ankle back together but it was touch and go for nerve repair. He may need some more surgery.'

This was easier. A professional kind of conversation.

'He's got external fixation, of course, and they're worried about infection. He's on a bucket of antibiotics and they think he'll be in hospital for at least a week. Quite possibly longer.'

'He'll be off work for quite a while, I expect.'

'Yes, but once he's home I'm sure they'll be able to cope without me as an extra parent.'

'What about you, Annie?' David's query was soft. 'Will *you* be able to cope with being an extra parent?'

'Yes.' Anne knew she sounded confident. She was. Any grief she might have felt about handing over the babies was well and truly lost in this new pain of losing David.

Again.

Julia came out of the living room, carrying the baby seats.

'Need some help?' David asked.

'I'm good. Thanks so much for everything, David.' Julia looked from him to her sister and a furrow of concern wrinkled her forehead. 'We'll be in the taxi,' she told Anne. 'No rush.'

'You didn't need to get a taxi. I would have taken you all home.'

'I know. But it would have been an hour's drive. It's after midnight and you've got an early start tomorrow. You've helped enough, David.'

His expression was guarded now. 'So it would seem.'

It was Anne's turn to leave but still she stood there, gripping the handle of her suitcase.

This was it. She was walking away from David and it would be for the last time. There would be no going back. The breath she tried to take in got stuck. She swallowed and tried again.

'I don't know what to say,' she whispered.

That she was sorry? That she'd been wrong? Would it help to tell him that Daniel hadn't needed her after all? That it had been bleeding from his spleen that had appeared to be under control but which had started again that had caused his deterioration? Another paediatric team had taken the little boy back to Theatre but by then Julia and Mac had arrived in the emergency department. Anyway, it had been the principle that had done the damage, not this specific incident or case.

'Don't say anything,' David suggested. 'The longer we spin this out, the more painful it's going to be for both of us.'

Anne hated that she was causing him pain. She could see it in his face. In the darkness of his eyes and the lines of strain. By the rigid way he was holding himself so still as he stood there.

'We were chasing the sun, Annie,' he said softly. 'It was inevitable that we would get burnt.'

No way could Anne stem the prickle at the back of her eyes or how tight her throat was now.

'I couldn't have got through the last couple of months if you hadn't been here.'

The tiny tremor of David's lips was the only sign that he was finding this as hard as she was.

'Hey…' His lips firmed and twisted into a rough smile. 'What are friends for?'

The handle of the case slipped from Anne's grasp and she stumbled forward, holding up her arms. David stepped into them and gathered her into the hug she needed so desperately.

But it was different.

She could feel his solidness and the circle his arms made around her. She could hear the thump of his heartbeat but it felt…distant.

Of course it did. He was protecting himself. From *her*.

It gave her a glimpse of this from his point of view. She'd been living a lie ever since he'd come back. He'd seen her pregnant. Giving birth, even. Being content to be away from her job and devoting herself to domestic pursuits like making a home and garden beautiful. She'd reeled him in by allowing their intimacy to re-kindle and grow.

And then she'd slapped him in the face when confronted by the choice of being with him and the babies—*family*—or doing her job.

Would he understand if she told him that she hadn't wanted to make the choice she'd been obliged to make? That it had broken her heart? But what difference would it make even if he did understand the cost? The knowledge that there would be lifetime of such conflict was more than enough to show them both that it could never have worked. That it would only have generated heartache and resentment.

That if children were involved, they would suffer too.

If she really loved David, she would let him go. Right now. She would set him free to get on with his life and have a family with someone who would adore him and let nothing get in the way of their time together.

She pulled back from his embrace. Trying to gather her strength so she could give David what he deserved.

'We'll always be friends, won't we?'

He had turned away. He was picking up her case.

Anne couldn't help rushing in to fill this

new silence. 'Maybe we could…have dinner or something. Before I go to Sydney. Or you go to London.'

David looked over his shoulder. He cleared his throat. 'We'll be friends, Annie, but I need a bit of space to get my head around things first.'

Of course he did. So did she. Anne followed him outside. This wound was far too raw to think of prodding it yet. It was still bleeding. Badly.

David handed her bag to the taxi driver and bent to smile at Julia who was in the back seat, flanked by her sleeping babies.

'Come and visit us soon,' she told him.

'Maybe.' The word was noncommittal. 'I'm going to be pretty busy. I don't want to let anyone down even if it is the last weeks of my locum. And I've got my work cut out for me if I want to get the house sold before I leave the country.'

And with no more than a nod at Anne, David was gone. As the taxi pulled out of the driveway, she saw the lights of the entranceway cut off as he closed the front door of his home behind him.

* * *

For the next ten days Anne's life was taken over by helping to care for the twins and keeping Julia's spirits up. There was the cooking and shopping and housework to take care of and a lot of time was spent travelling to and from hospital visits.

Being this busy was a blessing, however. Anne didn't have time to agonise over what had happened between herself and David and when she did finally fall into bed at night, she was too exhausted to do anything other than sleep.

Curiously, there was a peacefulness to be found amongst the hectic routine and that was the knowledge that she could help mother these babies and love them but they were not *hers*. She was able to live with them and care for them the same way she'd cared for her baby sister so many years ago. Recognising that, and remembering the power of the bond her body had shown her after giving birth, she had a glimpse of what it would be like to have her own child. One conceived in love, preferably with the father by her side.

Had she given away the only chance she might have to experience that? Chosen her career instead? It hadn't felt like a conscious choice at the time. She'd been doing her duty. The way she had all her life. Doing the right thing and earning points that would one day allow her to make her own choices.

This was supposed to be her time right now, wasn't it? And here she was doing her duty again and putting her own life on hold. She was living with the babies she'd given birth to. She was in a state of domesticity right up to her eyeballs. Dealing with bottles and nappies and crying babies. She wasn't getting enough sleep and it was just as stressful as she'd known it would be.

And she didn't want to be doing anything else.

How weird was that?

She hadn't seen David. The least she could give him was the space he'd requested. When they took the babies in to visit Mac, they would take the double pushchair with them and Anne would take the twins for a walk to give Julia some time alone with her husband. She would take them out the back of the hospital if the weather was nice and walk near the river. Well away from the emergency department and any chance of running into David.

It was hard enough to know that he came to visit Mac so often and that his news had been passed on until Julia had warned him that he was treading on painful ground. By then she already knew that David was looking forward to heading for London and that the marketing of his house was creating an enormous amount of interest. The agents were confident that the upcoming auction would be a huge success.

Mac did need a second operation on his ankle and by the following week the strain of the frequent visits were starting to show. It was a long drive, with difficult patches over the hills and winding around the bays.

'We've got to shift closer to town,' Julia said on one occasion, as they carried a pair of tired and hungry babies back into the house. 'We've been talking about it off and on since Mac went back to work after his paternity leave.'

'But you love this house. How could you sacrifice a view like this?'

'Family's more important,' Julia said quietly, lifting Angus from his car seat and kissing him. 'We knew Mac was losing family time with all the commuting and that we'd want to be closer to good schools and things when the twins were older. This accident has changed things. We talked about it today. The time we get together is just too precious to waste.'

Anne had picked Amy up. As comfortable with her aunt now as she was with her parents, Amy stopped grizzling and grinned. Anne smiled back, looked up to share the moment with Julia and found that her sister was watching her with an odd expression on her face.

'What?'

'Nothing.'

'Doesn't look like nothing.'

'I was just thinking, that's all. About priorities.'

'You mean do we change wet pants or make some formula first?'

Julia smiled. 'I was looking at a bigger picture. Thinking about how priorities change. That you can think you want something so much nothing else matters but then it changes. It doesn't have to get lost, it just gets…demoted, I guess.'

'You're talking about this house. The views, right? Demotion from an island in the harbour to a park in the city, yes?'

'Yeah…right.' But Julia's tone suggested that Anne was missing the point. That Julia had somehow overtaken her older sister in wisdom.

Maybe she had. Priorities were certainly getting juggled a little for Anne.

The planned month-long visit to the specialist paediatric hospital in Sydney was looming closer by the day but the desire to take advantage of the opportunity was fading at an even faster rate.

Finally, Anne sent an email. 'I'm sorry,' she

wrote, 'but, due to family circumstances, I'm no longer able to take this time away.'

Julia was shocked. 'But you've been looking forward to this for so long. It was all part of the plan after the babies were born.'

'You said it yourself,' Anne responded quietly. 'Priorities change. You need me right now.'

'Mac's coming home soon. We could cope.'

'I know you could but I *want* to help. This is where I need to be right now. Maybe I need you more than you need me.'

'Oh, hon.' Julia gathered her sister into her arms. 'I'm so sorry things haven't worked out for you and David. I wish there was something I could do.'

'Make me a coffee.' Anne smiled, blinking away tears. 'No…make that tea. I've gone right off coffee for the moment.' She pulled back and then did a double-take at her sister's expression. 'What?'

'That's exactly what you said just before you did your pregnancy test, remember?'

Anne laughed. 'I'm not pregnant again. It's not remotely possible. I'm not even ovulating again yet.'

'How do you know? Some women do it within a couple of weeks of giving birth.'

'I haven't had a period yet, that's how I know.'

Julia was giving her a very strange look. 'Well, you wouldn't, would you? If you were pregnant...'

Anne gave another amused snort. 'I'm not. Two babies is enough in this family. We decided against even the possibility of three way back at the implantation, remember?'

Julia reached for the kettle. 'I'm sure you're right. Just as well, eh? A baby of your own would be the last thing you want right now.'

'Mmm.' But Anne was staring through the window, not seeing the fabulous view of the harbour that Julia was prepared to give up for more important things. She was seeing a very different picture. A much bigger one.

* * *

'An iconic house,' the voice announced. 'A piece of our city's heritage that has been meticulously restored to its original glory. A real *family* home.'

From his upstairs bedroom window, David could look down onto the crowded lawn where the auction for this property was taking place on site. There had to be close to two hundred people here, he decided. Prospective buyers and curious onlookers. Agents who were flanking clients or had mobile phones pressed to their ears—in communication with more than one absent bidder who had registered their interest.

Strangers, all of them.

'Imagine entertaining in the glorious drawing room behind me,' the auctioneer continued. 'Looking out on this fabulous vista.'

David snorted, closing his eyes.

Impossible not to think of Anne. The way her eyes had danced with mischief when she'd been telling him the plans those landscape architects had had in mind for his garden.

'*Spheres*,' she'd said, amusement vying with primness.

'*Balls*,' he had countered.

He'd made her laugh and the sound had repaired a thread of connection between them.

The auctioneer had finally finished hyping up the crowd. 'Who wants to start the bidding?' he called.

David crossed the room to sit on the edge of his bed. He took a deep breath in through his nose but that was a mistake. Despite her absence and changing the linen more than once, he was sure he could still catch a hint of Anne's scent here. Not perfume. The scent of Anne. The one he'd filled his senses with that day on the beach when he'd kissed her for the first time in so long. He remembered the feeling of being poised on the edge of a cliff. In danger of falling into a crevasse he'd only just clawed his way clear of. He remembered feeling relieved when Anne had backed away.

Had he really thought he was still in control? That he could save himself from the kind of pain he was feeling now? He should have known he was lost when he'd gone home that day and thought she'd left. The flash of fear should have stopped him in his tracks but, no, he'd hurtled headlong into her arms pretty much, hadn't he?

Well, he had when he'd seen the way she'd looked at him when he'd told her about the pond. The way she had offered to help him retrieve something he'd lost long ago but still cared about.

He would have sworn he'd been able to see love in that look.

The kind of love he'd ached for.

But it had been doomed to failure. He should have known that. He did know it. Even if he gave up the dream of ever having a family, he would have to play second fiddle to Anne's career. There would be time after time when some emergency would take precedence. Like young Daniel that day, who'd fortunately come through the crisis and was apparently happily recuperating in the children's ward now.

He might have thought he was willing to accept

whatever crumbs of time were available with the juggling of two high-powered careers but it would be unfair on both of them to try. It was way too obvious where it would lead eventually. There would be resentment and guilt to begin with. And then they would drift apart, intent on their own paths through life. Without a family, the kind of glue that would make compromise a necessity would be missing.

Maybe he could make it work if he wanted it badly enough but Anne would have to want it just as much. Maybe he was just as much of an all-or-nothing personality as she was. But the 'all' he wanted was in his relationship. An equal commitment. To love and be loved in equal measure.

Was it really too much to ask?

Judging by the way Anne seemed to have been avoiding him ever since Mac's accident, apparently so.

The bidding from the crowd outside was heating up. Jumping higher in increments at such a speed

David hadn't noticing it passing the reserve he'd set before the auction had commenced.

'Folks…we *are on* the market,' the auctioneer boomed. 'Ladies and gentlemen, who is going to be the lucky family to enjoy this paradise with its country charm in the middle of city convenience? Who will have the pleasure of raising their children here? Or taking their grandchildren for a stroll to feed the fish in that fabulous pond?'

This shouldn't be happening. David shoved his fingers through his hair and then buried his face in his hands with a groan. He was cutting himself off from Anne. From their past. From his own childhood, even. He had no one to blame but himself. He was as selfish as he'd once accused Anne of being. Just as black and white. He'd told her she was incapable of compromise but had he ever actually tried to set a real example?

'*Sold!*' boomed a triumphant sound through the speaker system set up on the lawn. The sound of a gavel hitting the podium punctuated the finale.

Oh...God!

David's head snapped up. What had he done? What had he been *thinking*?

'*No!*' the word was uttered aloud and it was final. David got to his feet and strode out of the room.

'I'm not going to sell,' David told the startled group of real-estate personnel gathering in his hallway.

'But you already *have*,' the auctioneer insisted. 'It's a legal process, Dr Earnshaw. We have the new owner in the dining room, waiting to sign the contract.'

'I won't sign,' David said stubbornly.

'But why not?' The atmosphere of triumph around him was ebbing. Becoming alarmed. 'The price was more than any of us hoped for.'

'I've changed my mind,' David told him. 'Some things are far more important than money.'

'What kind of things?'

David's head turned at the sound of a feminine voice he knew so well.

'*Annie*…what are you doing here?'

'I came to watch the auction.' She edged through a gap in the group. 'It was a great price. Aren't you happy?'

'No.' David took a step closer to her. 'I'm not selling. This place represents my past. I want it to be part of my future as well.' He turned to glare at the auctioneer. 'You can say all you want about this being such a family home. About swings for children under the elm tree or grandchildren feeding the fish, but you know what?'

'What?' The auctioneer was eyeing him warily.

'It's not the number of people that make a family. It's about what holds them together. It's about *love*.'

'Of course it is.' An agent exchanged a meaningful look with the auctioneer and stepped forward. She had a sheaf of papers in her hand. Probably the sale-and-purchase agreement David was expected to sign. 'The new owners will love this property, I promise you.'

David ignored her. He turned back to Anne.

'I told you we were chasing the sun,' he said. 'And we got burned. I was going about it all wrong. You don't need to chase it. You just need to find a space where you can feel the warmth and see the light. I thought I had to shut myself away to keep safe but who wants to live in the dark?'

'Not me,' Anne said obligingly. The people around them were looking bemused but they shook their heads in agreement as well.

'I love you, Annie,' David said. 'I don't want to live without you. I don't care how big our family is. It's *you* I need.' He held out his hand. 'You're my sun. My warmth. My light.'

'Oh…David…' Anne had tears on her cheeks. 'That's all I ever needed to hear you say. I love you, too.'

'We'll work it out,' David promised, holding her close and kissing her.

'Of course you will,' said the auctioneer with a curiously gruff voice.

'We will,' Anne told him.

'I just need to sort out this mess first,' David groaned.

'What mess?'

'I'll have to find the person who thinks they're buying our home. I need to explain why they can't.'

'You just did.'

David blinked. He frowned at the auctioneer, who'd just spoken, and then looked to Anne's face smiling up at him. He was vaguely aware that everyone around them was also smiling. Grinning, even.

'You?' He blinked again. '*You* bought it?'

Anne nodded.

'Why?'

'It's a family home and…I want a family, David. With you.'

'But…'

'I was wrong. I thought I knew what I wanted but there I was, finally staring at what I thought was what I wanted, and it didn't look right. It looked empty. Like it was missing something really, really important.'

'Warmth?' David suggested softly. 'Light?'

'Heart,' Anne answered, standing on tiptoe to kiss David again. 'My heart. And you know why it wasn't there?'

'No. Why?'

'Because you have it.'

'And you have mine.' David managed to tear his gaze away from her for long enough to give their audience a firm stare. 'Would you all mind going away?' he asked politely. 'A man could do with a little privacy when he's about to propose.'

Anne watched everybody walking out of the hallway. She saw the auctioneer pull an enormous white handkerchief from his pocket and blow his nose with gusto.

She knew how he felt. Happy endings tended to have the same effect on her.

Except this wasn't an ending.

It was a beginning. For both of them. No, for all of them. Anne caught her breath. Should she tell David now that his dream of a family of his own was much closer than he could imagine?

He was about to propose. Too impatient to wait for everyone to clear the hallway completely, he had taken her hands and pulled her through the nearest doorway, which led into the biggest living area. He was looking down at her with such love in his face that Anne was lost. All she could do was bask in that love and wait for the chance to say 'yes'.

That she would marry him. Live with him and love him for the rest of her life.

There would be plenty of time to share the news of the baby. To make plans that would make it work for them all.

She'd been right after all. This *was* her time. Her chance to do exactly what she wanted most in her life.

'*Yes*,' she whispered.

'Oi!' David's tone was stern. 'I haven't asked yet.'

Anne smiled. 'Are you going to do the down-on-one-knee thing?'

'Good grief! Do you want me to?'

Her smile widened. 'Someone might appreciate it.'

David took his eyes off her for the first time since he'd brought her in here. He turned his head and realised where they were. Right in front of all the windows and French doors that led to the terrace and the lawn beyond. Some of the crowd had gone but there were still a lot of people out there and someone must have told them what was going on because they were all standing there quietly.

Watching. And smiling.

David grinned and went down on one knee. 'I love you, Anne Bennett,' he said. 'Will you marry me? Please?'

'Yes,' Anne said. And then, more loudly, in case her soft response hadn't been heard through the open doors, '*Yes*.'

The auctioneer blew his nose again. And then everyone started clapping.

EPILOGUE

SHE was the happiest woman in the world.

Jean MacCulloch paused for a moment longer in the bathroom, dampening her hand to smooth the grey corrugations of her newly permed hair. Then she pushed her wire-rimmed spectacles more firmly onto the bridge of her nose and went back outside to join her family.

Her family now. All of it.

She stopped on the terrace of this wonderful old house to admire the garden and soak in the party atmosphere. There were balloons everywhere. Rainbows of colour attached to tree branches and joined by twisted streamers. The shiny new red swing and slide set that was Emily Earnshaw's first birthday present was also adorned with decorations. Not that wee Emily was getting a chance to sit in the soft bucket seat of the swing because her cousins were making the most of their ten-month superiority in age.

'Me!' Angus was shouting. 'Me now!'

'No!' It was Amy's new favourite word. She was gripping the sides of the swing seat, resisting her mother's attempt at prying those little fingers loose. 'No!'

'One more swing,' Julia relented. 'But then it's definitely Angus's turn.'

Emily's parents were smiling at Julia losing the battle temporarily. Anne was busy arranging a party picnic afternoon tea on the child-sized table and chairs that had been set up on the lawn. Pretty cup cakes with pastel icing and marshmallow butterflies on top. Gingerbread people with bright candy-covered chocolate buttons. Platters of fresh fruit pieces and plastic tumblers of juice. There was a cake, too, of course. Pink and white with pretty pink bows and icing flowers and a single candle.

David was holding his tiny daughter who looked every inch the birthday princess in a ruffled pink dress with white socks and sandals and a soft pink headband with a bow to hold back golden curls that were just getting long enough to get in her eyes.

'What do you think, Emily?' he asked, lifting the little girl so that she was in the air looking down at her father. 'Is Amy being a wee bit naughty?'

Emily gurgled with laughter and waved chubby fists.

'Mac!' Julia was trying not to laugh as Amy thwarted new efforts to unclamp her fingers. 'Do something…'

But Mac had spotted his mother and was almost at the terrace steps. 'You all right, Mum?'

'Never better, lad,' Jean assured him. She met him at the bottom of the steps.

'Not too much for you? All these noisy little people?'

Jean smiled. 'It doesn't seem that long ago that you were one of them, Alan MacCulloch. And look at you now.' She had to look a long way up. 'I do wish you'd stop growing.'

Mac laughed and drew her towards the swing.

Jean walked slowly. Not because she didn't have more than enough energy but because she wanted to make this moment last a little longer.

'Do you remember when I came to visit with Doreen when you and Julia were first married?'

'Aye. Of course I do.'

'I was so happy for you both but Doreen was trying to spoil it for me. Lording it over me, she was, all the way back to Glasgow, and you know what a long trip *that* is.'

'I certainly do.' Mac was frowning. 'What was Doreen doing to spoil things?'

'Oh, you know, going on and on about how wonderful her Lachlan's family was. Saying that, of course, Julia was a wonderful lassie but wasn't it the greatest shame that you'd never have any bairns? That I'd never be a grandmother?' Doreen clicked her tongue. 'If only I'd known then what Anne had offered as your wedding gift.'

'We didn't tell you because it took us a long

time to decide to accept it. It was all too amazing, really.'

'Aye,' Jean said softly. 'So it was. And now I *am* a grandmother. To the bonniest wee bairns in the world.'

'I'll bet that put Doreen's nose out of joint.'

'Aye. And then I told her that I was going to come out here to live.'

'What did she say to that?'

'That I needed my head read. That I was too old to be helping to raise babies and being an adopted grandmother to your wee ones' cousin was just plain daft.'

'You don't mind, though, do you? You're the closest thing to a gran that wee Emily is ever going to have.'

'I'm thrilled, lad. You're all like one family, anyway, what with Julia looking after all the babies on the days that Anne and David are both working.'

'Dadda!' Angus had forgotten he was waiting his turn for the swing. 'Pick me up, Dadda.'

'No,' Amy cried. 'Me!' She gave up the battle

to stay in the seat and lifted both arms so that Julia could lift her out. Then she toddled as fast as she could towards Mac, leaving Julia shaking her head.

David had put Emily down. She was standing in front of him and he was holding both her hands. Tentatively, the birthday girl stepped towards her mother who had finished setting out the picnic and was kneeling on the grass, her arms outstretched.

'Look at you.' Anne beamed. '*Clever* girl, Em.'

Mac had a toddler attached to each leg and was moving, with difficulty, towards Anne and the table.

'Food, guys,' he told his children. 'Look… cake!'

Julia caught up with Jean and they both followed, smiling.

David let go of one of Emily's hands when she was close to her mother. Then he let go of the other one. For three whole steps Emily managed to stay upright and then Anne caught her. She cuddled and kissed her daughter but was looking up at her husband to share the joy of the moment.

'Time to light the candle,' David said. 'I reckon we can all make a wish.'

'I don't have anything to wish *for*,' Anne said. I'm the happiest woman on earth.'

Julia was watching Mac as he gave up and sat down on the lawn to let the twins clamber on top of him.

'No,' she said quietly. 'I think I am.'

'Nonsense,' Jean said firmly. '*I* am.' She gazed around at her newly extended family. 'Look at you all.' She beamed. 'And here I am instead of being thousands of miles away. No one could be happier than me.'

But no-one seemed to be listening. Mac had a small child under each arm and he was looking up at Julia, sharing a smile that excluded everyone else.

Anne and David were smiling at each other, too, over the blonde curls of their daughter.

Secret smiles. Full of the kind of love that

could make anyone feel like the happiest person in existence.

Jean's nod was satisfied. She was getting to share it all and she knew she was right.

She was definitely the happiest woman in the world.

MEDICAL™

Large Print

Titles for the next six months…

March

DATING THE MILLIONAIRE DOCTOR	Marion Lennox
ALESSANDRO AND THE CHEERY NANNY	Amy Andrews
VALENTINO'S PREGNANCY BOMBSHELL	Amy Andrews
A KNIGHT FOR NURSE HART	Laura Iding
A NURSE TO TAME THE PLAYBOY	Maggie Kingsley
VILLAGE MIDWIFE, BLUSHING BRIDE	Gill Sanderson

April

BACHELOR OF THE BABY WARD	Meredith Webber
FAIRYTALE ON THE CHILDREN'S WARD	Meredith Webber
PLAYBOY UNDER THE MISTLETOE	Joanna Neil
OFFICER, SURGEON…GENTLEMAN!	Janice Lynn
MIDWIFE IN THE FAMILY WAY	Fiona McArthur
THEIR MARRIAGE MIRACLE	Sue MacKay

May

DR ZINETTI'S SNOWKISSED BRIDE	Sarah Morgan
THE CHRISTMAS BABY BUMP	Lynne Marshall
CHRISTMAS IN BLUEBELL COVE	Abigail Gordon
THE VILLAGE NURSE'S HAPPY-EVER-AFTER	Abigail Gordon
THE MOST MAGICAL GIFT OF ALL	Fiona Lowe
CHRISTMAS MIRACLE: A FAMILY	Dianne Drake

MILLS & BOON

MEDICAL™

Large Print

MILLS & BOON